EDGE: BLOOD RUN

Other books by this author available from New English Library:

EDGE 1: THE LONER
EDGE 2: TEN THOUSAND DOLLARS AMERICAN
EDGE 3: APACHE DEATH
EDGE 4: KILLER'S BREED
EDGE 5: BLOOD ON SILVER
EDGE 6: THE BLUE THE GREY AND THE RED
EDGE 7: CALIFORNIA KILLING
EDGE 8: SEVEN OUT OF HILL
EDGE 9: BLOODY SUMMER
EDGE 10: VENGEANCE IS BLACK
EDGE 11: SIOUX UPRISING
EDGE 12: THE BIGGEST BOUNTY
EDGE 13: A TOWN CALLED HATE
EDGE 14: THE BIG GOLD
EDGE 16: THE FINAL SHOT
EDGE 17: VENGEANCE VALLEY
EDGE 18: TEN TOMBSTONES TO TEXAS
EDGE 19: ASHES AND DUST
EDGE 20: SULLIVAN'S LAW
EDGE 21: RHAPSODY IN RED
EDGE 22: SLAUGHTER ROAD
EDGE 23: ECHOES OF WAR
EDGE 24: THE DAY DEMOCRACY DIED

ADAM STEELE 1: THE VIOLENT PEACE
ADAM STEELE 2: BOUNTY HUNTER
ADAM STEELE 3: HELL'S JUNCTION
ADAM STEELE 4: VALLEY OF BLOOD
ADAM STEELE 5: GUN RUN
ADAM STEELE 6: THE KILLING ART
ADAM STEELE 7: CROSS-FIRE
ADAM STEELE 8: COMANCHE CARNAGE
ADAM STEELE 9: BADGE IN THE DUST
ADAM STEELE 10: THE LOSERS
ADAM STEELE 11: LYNCH TOWN
ADAM STEELE 12: DEATH TRAIL
ADAM STEELE 13: BLOODY BORDER
ADAM STEELE 14: DELTA DUEL
ADAM STEELE 15: RIVER OF DEATH

Edge: Blood Run

GEORGE G. GILMAN

NEW ENGLISH LIBRARY
TIMES MIRROR

for B.G.
who is so important to the production of Edge

An NEL Original
First published in hardcover as DOUBLE ACTION together with
Adam Steele: VALLEY OF BLOOD in 1974.

*

FIRST NEL PAPERBACK EDITION FEBRUARY 1975
This new edition January 1978

*

NEL Books are published by The New English Library Limited from Barnard's Inn, Holborn, London EC1N 2JR. Made and printed in Great Britain by C. Nicholls & Company Ltd

45003746 0

AUTHOR'S NOTE

Although complete in itself, this book continues the Civil War adventures of the man now called Edge. Previous books in this flashback sequence are *Killer's Breed*, *The Blue*, *The Grey And The Red*, *Seven Out Of Hell*, *Vengeance is Black* and *The Biggest Bounty*.

CHAPTER ONE

THE clouds hung so low they seemed to scrape the jagged tops of the cliffs on either side of the rushing water that crashed and broiled towards its meeting place with the Columbia River twenty miles to the north. They were dark grey, shading to near full-black in patches and streaks, and were racing southwards ahead of a spiteful wind that howled louder than the roar of the white water as it funnelled into the narrowing neck of the gorge.

Where the cliff faces tapered and almost touched, they provided towering banks to contain the angry water. But downstream where the gorge widened there was a natural step, of rock in some places and grass-covered earth in others, at the foot of each cliff. Mixed timber of willow, ash, oak and pine thrived along the earthy sections of the banks and it was through the leafless branches of a knarled oak that the man called Edge looked down at the men who would die within an hour—unless he helped them.

There were two of them, with their arms lashed to their sides and their legs bound at knees and ankles. They were strung, upside-down, by lengths of rope hitched around the lowest branch of the oak and tied to their ankles. One of the men was at least six inches shorter than the other, but the ropes had been cut so that both their heads were an equal few inches above the fast-flowing water.

They seemed to have been suspended thus for a long time, but it was not until the half-breed reined his big stallion to a halt at the rim of the gorge's east cliff that their helplessness became desperate. For it was at that moment that the scudding clouds delivered their threat and unleashed a cascade of teeming rain.

"Oh, Jesus Christ Almighty, Gabby!" the shorter of the two screamed in panic. "Them crazy bastards got their damn prayers answered. We're gonna die!"

It would take time for the stream to swell with new rain, but in his terrified imagination the man was certain he was on the verge of instant drowning. He forced his head up and struggled desperately to arch his back and hold the position. His complexion, already crimson from the pressure of blood to his head, shaded to deep purple with the exertion.

"Quit it, Estes," the other man growled in a voice larded with the same brand of hillbilly accents as his partner in trouble. "Or could be you'll die of the heart strain 'fore the water gets you."

Estes could not hold the muscle-stretching posture any longer and he flopped back to the loose-hanging position. The branch creaked ominously and bowed. The ropes turned and the men spun slowly at their ends. Spume from partially submerged rocks reinforced the raindrops beating against their faces.

"And quit bouncin' up and down, lunkhead!" Gabby snarled. "Maybe you're in a rush to die, but I ain't, that's for sure."

The branch returned to its natural growing angle and the ropes ceased to turn. The men glared at each other's distorted, upside-down faces across a space of three feet. Edge eyed them coldly through lids narrowed against the wind and rain, able to hear each word they said before the spring storm whipped their voices into infinity.

"What difference does it make?" Estes demanded. "Pat was the lucky one. For him it was quick." He injected scorn into his tone. "Might as well drown now. Unless you got somethin' important you wanna do before you cash in your chips?"

"Maybe get away and live a few more years," Gabby answered. "And teach them God-crazy guys not to fool with Silas Gabb."

Estes tried to spit into the stream, but the wind eddied and flung the saliva back into his blood-heavy face. He cursed. "You figure the Man upstairs'll listen to your prayers?" he growled.

"Prayin' I got no time for," Gabb yelled above the crash of water and roar of wind. "Luck, I have. And it's time mine changed."

"Fat chance!" Estes taunted, and timed the spit better this time.

"He don't look so fat to me," Gabb replied, and locked stares with Edge.

Estes had started to concentrate upon a patch of brush growing out from the side of the bank beneath the tree: trying to gauge the rate of the rising water in relation to the lowest clump of foliage. But the flow was broken by bed rocks and the brush moved constantly in the tug of the wind. Then something in the flat tone of Gabb's voice penetrated his fear and he snapped his head around to follow the direction of his partner's gaze. He had to look upwards—along the length of his suspended form, through the branches of the oak and then across the grey rock face of the eastern cliff. At first, excitement at the sight of Edge choked him. But then he cleared his throat.

"Damn it to hell, Gabby!" he yelled. "We're gonna get saved." Then he raised his voice higher, shouting loud enough to make the blood-vessels stand out, like blue ropes, against his neck and temples. "Hey, you up there! Hey mister! Give us a hand, uh? Mister, please!"

Gabb and the half-breed continued to eye each other. "Estes!" Gabb called, just loud enough to be heard above the sounds of angry nature.

"Yeah, Gabby?" Estes showed his tobacco-stained and time-decayed teeth in a broad grin.

"The guy's seen us. He's seen the fix we're in. He either comes down here or he don't. You hollerin' like a stuck pig ain't gonna make any difference one way or the other."

Still he continued to crane up his head to look at the top of the cliff. And still Edge did not move, held in stark black silhouette against the wet-sheened, fast-moving greyness of the rain clouds. Man and horse seemed to be carved out of black marble for long moments. Then, with a slight movement of his heels and a gentle tug on the reins, Edge wheeled his horse away from the cliff top and went from sight.

"The bastard's leavin' us!" Estes screamed hysterically.

"A hundred feet straight down into maybe three feet of water?" Gabb pointed out sourly.

Once more the taller man's calm logic drove Estes back from the brink of despair and both twisted their heads to the side. To look downstream, cracking their eyes against the wind and rain pummelling their faces. That was the direction in which Edge had turned his horse and although it was difficult to see much through the driving downpour, both men knew what the terrain was like to the north. For that was the way they had been brought to their place of slow execution.

The gorge petered out after three hundred yards or so, the cliffs veering away to the sides and losing height rapidly to crumble into boulderstrewn, wooded slopes. Beyond was a broad valley, heavily timbered, with the stream curving across it and widening to the proportions of a river. Then, as the valley and river made a dog-leg swing to the north-west, the foundations of the cathedral and the strange town came into view.

"Sure as hell is takin' his time, Gabby," Estes complained after a few minutes had seemed to stretch into hours.

"His privilege," Gabb answered and although his tone remained colder than the wind-driven rain, there was just a trace of anxiety in his upside-down face.

Then a look of intense concentration entered his slitted eyes and his head craned forward. A shadow moved in the murky curtain of rain on the same bank of the stream as the oak tree. A moment later the shadow took shape and substance: a tall man astride a big horse. Hooves clattered on rock and thudded against grass. Edge reined his horse to a halt beneath the insecure umbrella of the oak.

"Lousy weather to have to hang around in," he greeted evenly, and swung out of the saddle.

"Lousy time to make jokes!" Estes rasped.

"Quit it, lunkhead!" Gabb snarled, fixing the half-breed with an inquiring stare as he mentally swung around his upside-down image of the newcomer.

He saw a man more than just tall—maybe six feet three inches —who looked to weigh close to two hundred pounds: a lot of it muscle and bone with no excess fat. But in the back of his lean, angular features with the light blue eyes, hawkish nose, high cheekbones, narrow mouth above a firm jaw—the whole stretched over with deeply-lined, burnished brown skin—was more than a hint that his head was not just muscle and bone. He looked to be in his mid-thirties and he also looked to have the blood of two races coursing through his veins. Mexican for sure. And European—northern European, Gabb guessed. His dress was dark-hued and ill-suited to the chill of Oregon in the transition of the seasons from Winter to Spring. A black, low-crowned hat from which blacker hair swept down to brush the shoulders of his grey cotton shirt, open at the neck to show a length of whipcord strung with beads. His pants were of dark denim, the cuffs draped outside ancient riding boots. He wore a weathered gunbelt fully stocked with shells supporting a holster tied down to the right thigh. A standard Colt six-shooter without trimmings jutted from the cracked leather. The stock of a Winchester angled from the saddleboot.

Although his stance and expression were casual as he surveyed the predicament of the two men, there was something about the look of him which suggested he was quick to ice-cold anger: and fast to react to his impulses.

He crouched down and tipped his head to one side, on a level with and getting a less distorted view of the faces of the hanging men. "Upset someone, uh?" he asked.

"Took more than just some*one* to string us up like this, mister!" Estes rasped. He was about five feet seven inches tall and thickset with a squarish head and a face that had a pleasant but unintelligent cast with dull-looking brown eyes and a weak jawline, a crookedly broken nose and a loose mouth. He was about forty.

"But wouldn't take no more than the one of you to cut us down," Gabb augmented, his tone unruffled. "Name's Silas Gabb. This here's my partner, Estes Mackinlay."

Gabb was a few years the elder and a head taller. Much heavier, with wide shoulders, a broad chest and a hard-looking, narrow waistline. His face was more thickly stubbled than

Mackinlay's, with ruggedly handsome features: clear grey eyes, finely sculptored nose and well-formed mouth above a solid jaw. Their set suggested a brooding nature and he looked like a man who did not smile often.

Both men had thinning black hair and wore identical outfits: buck-skin pants tucked into knee-high leather boots and fur-lined tunics buttoned over buck-skin shirts with bandanas knotted at their throats.

"Get called Edge most of the time," the squatting half-breed replied. "Some other times I'm called a bastard." His thin lips drew back to show even teeth in a cold grin. But his eyes, blue as a summer sky at dawn, fixed Mackinlay with a stare completely devoid of humour.

"You heard me, uh?" Mackinlay rasped, and swallowed hard. "I was mad, mister. That's all. Figured you was gonna ride off and leave us. That thought didn't give me no peace of mind."

"Estes always gettin' into trouble on account of his temper, Edge," Gabb excused. "Hope you'll forgive him."

"Forgiving's no problem," Edge said as he straightened up, lifting a hand to the back of his neck. The beaded cord held a buck-skin pouch at the nape, pointing down the line of his spine. In the pouch was a cut-throat razor he had won long ago in a far off war.* Its blade had a subdued sheen in the dull storm light as the weapon was drawn clear of the long hair. "It's forgetting gives the trouble—to other people."

He stepped down from the bank and waded sure-footed out to where the two men were hanging. The rushing water slapped into his legs and sprayed the faces of the men.

"Mister . . . !" Mackinlay pleaded, his features contorted by fear as he looked up at the face of the half-breed.

"My folks were married," the half-breed said. "In a church with my mother dressed in white and me just a hope in her heart."

"Like Gabby said, mister," Mackinlay blubbered, tearing his eyes away from Edge's cold grin to stare in horror at the razor. "I got this lousy temper. I get mad easy."

**See—Edge: Killer's Breed.*

Edge closed down the grin to purse his lips. Then he made a cross-wise slash with the razor. The finely-honed blade sliced through the rope suspending Mackinlay. The man screamed and plunged into the white water. It was a short-lived scream and then his gurgling was muted by all the other sounds in the storm-lashed gorge. The half-breed's solidly placed splayed legs prevented the helpless man from being dragged downstream by the current.

"Get him outta the water for Christ's sake!" Gabb yelled. "The lunkhead'll drown."

"Cool his temper and keep his mouth shut for awhile, is all," Edge answered evenly. Then the razor slashed three times more, all the cuts in a downward direction. The first sliced through the ropes holding Gabb's arms against his sides. The second severed the bonds at his knees. The third bit through the rope trapping his ankles and holding him to the tree branch. Arms and hands which had been starved of circulation for so long could make only a token attempt to break the man's head-first plunge into the icy water.

Edge slid the razor back into its pouch then swung around and waded to the bank. Behind him, Gabb struggled to sit up against the rush of water and managed to snatch Mackinlay to him before the deluge dragged him away. He forced his partner's head above the surface and both men sucked in great gulps of air. Edge stepped up on to the bank and narrowed his eyes against the slanting rain.

"Ain't exactly picnic weather out there," he called evenly. "But the talking'll be easier if we don't have to shout at each other."

"You're mighty sparing with your help, mister!" Gabb accused, struggling to his feet and starting to haul Mackinlay towards the bank.

"Only give as much as I need to get what I want," Edge answered, crouching down and taking out the makings from his shirt pocket. He rolled the cigarette in the restricted dry space beneath the belly of his black stallion. He used the same sheltered area to light it and when he turned around, Gabb had dragged his partner up on to the bank. Both men were still gulping in air as their bodies shuddered with cold, like freshly landed fish.

"We ain't got a thing to give," Gabb told the half-breed sourly as he began to work on Mackinlay's bonds with shaking fingers. "Just the clothes we're wearin' is all."

"Not my style," Edge said, moving in close to the thick trunk of the oak, on the side away from the driving rain. "Trappers, uh?"

"Now we're trappers," Gabb answered. "We done dirt-farming in Kentucky, cattle driving in Texas, raised wheat in Kansas, prospected in California and Mexico, fought in the war between the States . . . You name it, we done it. For more than twenty years we been together."

"I need your life stories as much as I want your threads," Edge said, relishing the cigarette.

"So what else?" Gabb asked.

"Information."

"Tell you all we can if I can have the loan of your razor, mister," the taller trapper offered as he continued to struggle with the first knot. Weak from the long period of hanging from the tree, he had caught a chill from the soaking. The rain and wind weren't helping and his whole body was attacked by a spasm of trembling.

"I do that, I've got nothing to bargain with, feller," Edge told him, shielding the cigarette in a cupped hand.

Gabb's rugged, stubbled face showed he didn't like the answer. But a sigh of resignation admitted his inability to alter the situation. He gave up working on the knots and half rose. Mackinlay seemed to want to say something, but whenever he unclamped his mouth, the discoloured upper and lower teeth rattled against each other. Gabb grasped him under the armpits and dragged him into the sparse shelter offered beneath the downwind foliage of the oak tree.

Then he squatted on his haunches and crossed his arms across his chest to hug his shoulders. "Wouldn't say no to a cigarette," he rasped.

"Didn't make you the offer," Edge told him flatly. "I cut you down and maybe you'll get the means to loose your partner. But I wouldn't want you to get too deep into debt before I knew you could cover it."

He had smoked only half the cigarette. Deliberately, he flicked the butt out into the wind and rain. The ash was extinguished immediately and the paper and tobacco became a sopping, disintegrated mess almost as soon as it hit the grass.

"You're an easy man to hate, mister," Gabb growled.

"In my book it's what makes me so popular," the half-breed answered. "You want to start making payment on that loan now?"

"How?"

"Tell me what I don't have to do to keep from getting trussed up and hung out in the rain?"

"Easy," Gabb answered. "Stay clear of Paradise."

Edge's lips curled back to show his teeth in a mirthless grin. "Most people figure I'm headed in the opposite direction."

Gabb spat on to the ground between his knees and nodded downstream. "The Paradise I'm talkin' about is for the livin'," he said dully. "Couple of miles along the valley to the north."

"If you can call what them God-crazy folks do there livin'," Mackinlay managed to stutter between his chattering teeth.

"Name of a town," Gabb went on. "Only town in this neck of the woods."

Edge shook his head. "Then it ain't easy, feller. My horse needs shoeing and decent feed. And I need supplies."

"You asked and I told you," Gabb growled.

"You did more than visit the store in town," Edge accused evenly.

Gabb tried to hold the half-breed's steady, blue-eyed gaze but couldn't make it. He shook his head and rose from the squat. "Look, we didn't do nothin' that would have riled up ordinary folks in an ordinary town," he said quickly, holding the windblown hair away from his eyes. "I told you to stay away from Paradise and that's all you gotta do to keep clear of trouble in these parts."

Edge took more tobacco and a paper from his pocket and used

his body as a shield to keep off the rain as he rolled a cigarette. He lit it, aware of Gabb's malevolent stare. But then the trapper showed an awkward, unpractised grin as the cigarette was handed to him in long, brown fingers. Then Edge crouched, drew the razor and sliced through the ropes binding Mackinlay.

"Last town I was in, they hanged a man for spitting in the street," he said conversationally.*

"Sounds like you been to Paradise already, mister," Gabb replied in the same tone, more at ease now he had got both his requirements filled.

"All we done was talk to a couple of girls," Mackinlay supplied, his mood improved by the new freedom. But he was still weak and in pain and had to rub his body vigorously before he could stagger to his feet.

Edge slid the razor back into the neck pouch and narrowed his eyes as a slight movement disturbed the natural pattern of falling rain on the periphery of his vision.

"Just talk is all," Mackinlay continued, loosing the stutter with a struggle and talking unnaturally fast. "Passin' the time of day as you might say. Me and Gabby and this guy Pat O'Rerry we teamed up with couple of weeks ago. Just funnin' the dames. Then, like from nowhere, these God-crazy guys moved in on us with irons like I ain't never seen before. Real wild guys. We figured we was goin' to get blasted right there and then."

"You mean like now?" the half-breed asked, just loud enough to be heard above the storm. He had not seen a signal pass between the two trappers. But, since they had been partners for so long, it was possible no sign was necessary. It could be that when they were in trouble they acted in unison with an instinctive understanding of what each was required to do. Edge, as Lieutenant, then Captain, Josiah C. Hedges of the Federal Cavalry, had survived a war because of such a rapport developed with the six men who formed the nucleus of his command.

"What?" Mackinlay croaked.

"Like you'll get blasted now if your buddy moves another inch towards my horse."

**See—Edge: A Town Called Hate.*

He saw the shock of discovery freeze on Mackinlay's face. Then he whirled, corkscrewing down into a half-crouch. His right hand moved in a blur, fingers curling and thumb hooked. The Colt came clear of the holster, thumb cocking the hammer and index finger taking first pressure around the trigger.

Gabb was like a carved statue for a split-second. He was on his toes, leaning to one side. His left arm was bent in front of him, the hand in process of taking the cigarette from his lips. The other was stretched to its fullest extent, fingers clawed to grip the steel frame of the Winchester and draw it from the boot.

The tall trapper caught his breath as the Colt levelled at his heart. When he snapped open his mouth to yell, the wind snatched away the cigarette in a shower of sparks that stung his eyes. Then the Colt raked away from its fatal aim. The single shot was repeated time and time again on a diminishing note, resounding between the rearing rock faces of the gorge. The final echoes were drowned out by the genuine scream and the bouncing imitations. Gabb's agonised gaze was held for a split-second by the ice-cold gleam in the half-breed's piercing eyes. Then he looked along the length of his outstretched arm and saw the hole drilled through the palm of his clawed hand. The wind captured the gouting blood and hurled it up the gorge in a fine spray. Then he fisted the hand and folded the arm, bringing the wound to his lips to suck at the blood.

Edge's crouching form whirled again, and Mackinlay stumbled backwards, away from the menace of the revolver muzzle as it drew a bead on him.

"I didn't do nothin', mister!" he yelled in terror.

"Just talk is all," Edge repeated the man's words of a few moments ago. "Called creating a diversion. Helping your partner. But I guess that wasn't the kind of hand he was hoping to get."

"Please, mister!" Mackinlay begged. "We got nothing. Those crazy people in Paradise took our guns, our horses, our supplies . . . we ain't got nothin' . . . "

"Quit it!" Gabb snapped, allowing his injured hand to fall

from his face as he craned his head forward in a listening attitude.

The moment Mackinlay's words were cut in mid-sentence, he and Edge heard the new sound, too. Distant at first, but swelling by the moment against the angry noises of the storm: the beat of many hooves as a group of horsemen galloped their mounts into the mouth of the gorge. Abruptly, the smaller trapper's fear of the levelled Colt was swamped by a greater terror. And the shudder which rocked him from head to toe had nothing to do with the cold and damp.

"I'm leavin'," he shrieked at Edge, like a challenge for the half-breed to shoot him.

Then he powered into a run—taking the only course open to him to escape the swelling volume of the beating hooves. He raced upstream: on the bank until the sheer walls of the gorge closed in, then plunging into the rushing water.

"I've got good cause to remember you, mister!" Gabb snarled, brandishing his bleeding right hand in the air as though it were a weapon. "And I'll see you pay for this."

"Guess you've got a bloody right," Edge muttered.

Then Gabb whirled and sprinted in pursuit of his partner. His gait was awkwardly lopsided, with his injured hand held low at his side. The handicap of the wound was even more apparent when he plunged into the waist-deep stream. The moment he stepped off the bank, he was almost knocked off his feet by the power of the white water sweeping through the narrows. But friendship for Gabb transcended Mackinlay's terror of the approaching horsemen and selfish desire for escape. Braced against the rocky wall, he reached back and clasped the taller man's outstretched good hand. Then, leaning into the surge of angry water, he plunged forward, dragging Gabb in his wake.

Edge watched them out of sight amid the driving rain and flying spume, expecting at any moment to see them reappear—hurled into view like pieces of inanimate, storm-tossed driftwood. But the only trace of them he saw was a faint pinkish tint in the broiling, bubbling whiteness of the rushing, crashing water.

Perhaps blood from the hole in Gabb's hand or maybe from a larger, rock-inflicted wound.

Then, as the thunder of hooves filled the gorge, masking all other sounds, the half-breed turned to watch the bunch of a dozen riders rein their snorting, rearing horses to a halt. He looked at them through hooded eyes, his lips set in a quizzical line. The cocked revolver was held loosely at his side, pointing at the sodden ground. Before the final echo of the stamping, skidding, snorting halt had faded, the horsemen jostled into further movement. Well-schooled animals complied instantly to the demands of heel pressure and the tightening of reins. Within moments, during which not a word was spoken, the men had broken out of the tight-knit group and formed into a line blocking the mouth of the gorge. On both banks and in the rushing water of the stream, the horses stood stock-still. Their riders were as stoically unmoving. Twelve pairs of eyes stared blankly at Edge.

"What has become of the two sinners who were left here to suffer the punishment of the Lord?"

The speaker was directly in front of Edge and ten feet away from him. He was a tall, grey-faced man with sunken cheeks and hollow eyes. His skin was scored with deep lines, cut through more than sixty years. His hair was stark white, the utter purity of the lack of colour perhaps owing something to the vivid contrast with the solid blackness of his clothing. Stovepipe hat held on against the wind with a chinstrap, bootlace tie, shirt, calf-length frock coat, pants and boots were all as black as a raven's plummage. Every man was dressed in identical garb. And their weapons were also of a pattern: each carried an ancient .54 Starr muzzle loader with a 36-inch barrel. It was a model familiar to Edge, for one such gun had belonged to his Mexican father and had hung above the mantelshelf in the Iowa farmhouse before the spread was burned to the ground*.

Each strangely attired, impassive-faced man held his musket one-handed slanting across the front of his body, leaning against a thrust-forward shoulder. The posture was neutral but suggested a latent threat of aggression.

**See—Edge: The Loner.*

"The Lord took his time," Edge replied evenly. "I got here first."

The white-haired man dropped his steady gaze from Edge's face to the severed ropes which had been cut from Mackinlay's body. "You set the sinners free?" he intoned in his oddly resonant voice.

"We made a trade," Edge told him. "One good turn deserves another."

"A man who aids a sinner is equally a culprit in the eyes of the Lord." As the white-haired man spoke, he snapped the ancient Starr to the aim, gripping it two-handed. His fingers looked like skin-hung bone with no flesh between.

The other men were only a moment later in levelling their muskets at the half-breed. But in that sliver of time, Edge had brought up the Colt to draw a bead on the heart of the white-haired man.

"Killing's a sin, feller," Edge said. "You'll pay for the whole bundle. Maybe one other."

The aged face of the group's leader lost its blankness as the corner of his mouth took on a nervous twitch. And the confidence had drained from his voice. "We are the Earthly Angels of the town of Paradise," he croaked. "We are not people of violence. You may pass in peace."

He lowered the musket, turned in his saddle and thrust it into the boot. The others followed his example.

"Something you ought to know," Edge said flatly, still pointing the Colt at the white-haired man: not trusting the fast back-down.

"Yes, sinner?"

Facing into the wind, Edge spat from the corner of his mouth. The globule of saliva was whipped past the side of his head. "Names, I sometimes let ride. But the biggest mistake a man can make is to point a gun at me and not squeeze the trigger. Because I only make allowances for one mistake."

He let his arm drop, thumb easing the hammer back to the rest as he slid the Colt into the holster.

"Threats do not frighten the Arch Angel Luke!" a man at the

far left of the line called. "Nor any of us. Whatever happens, it is the will of the Lord."

"Reckon it's His will I get supplies and feed and shoes for my horse in Paradise?" the half-breed asked.

Luke backed his horse out of the line to leave a gap. He beckoned an invitation for Edge to pass through. Watchful, the half-breed turned the stallion around, then swung into the saddle. But he held the horse to a standstill and shook his head.

"Obliged, Luke," he said, showing his teeth in a humourless grin. "But I ain't rushing in to act like a fool with this bunch of angels backing me. You guys take the lead."

The corners of his thin mouth turned up in secret amusement as the theatrical analogy struck him. And then his expression hardened once more when his memory flipped forward a recollection from the violent past: of an impromptu dramatic performance which led to him and six others being the first Union soldiers to enter the Confederate capital of Richmond.

Luke shrugged his thin shoulders and wheeled his horse, beckoning his men to fall in behind him. "As you wish, sinner."

"Big of you to see things from my point of view, feller," Edge called. "Just that I wouldn't want to die the death—what with all these Starrs around."

CHAPTER TWO

It was in the April of 1864 when Captain Josiah C. Hedges surrendered himself and his six Union calvalry troopers to the custody of the Rebels. The time was after midnight and the place was the office of Jefferson Davis, President of the breakaway Confederate states.*

The Civil War had dragged bloodily on for almost four years and it had seemed like a brilliant idea when, at a Chiefs of Staff meeting in Washington, somebody suggested the assassination of Davis as a means to bring about a speedy end. Whether or not the theory had been brilliant, the assassination attempt had been put into practice. And seven men had slaughtered and connived their way to within a hairs breadth of success. But, because of that narrowest of margins, the seven tasted the bitter opposite of success—rank failure.

Now, on the day that the Rebels recaptured Fort Pillow in Tennessee and General Ulysses S. Grant first mooted his intention to halt prisoner exchanges to reduce Confederate manpower, the seven were escorted into Richmond's Riverside Prison. They knew nothing of what was happening in the theatres of war far beyond the non-combat zone of the Rebel capital. And even had they been aware of Grant's decision it would have been of no concern to them. For they had been captured in the Capitol Building while wearing civilian clothing: and were thus regarded as spies rather than soldiers. They had no military rights: and, in addition, the seriousness of their abortive mission called for swift retribution. There had not even been a summary trial—a secretary had filled out the names on the seven execution orders

**See—Edge: The Biggest Bounty.*

and a grim-faced Jefferson Davis had scrawled his signature on them. The manner of death was specified as hanging and the time set for dawn.

It was two o'clock in the misty morning when the fully-enclosed carriage drawn by a four-horse team swung in through the gates of the prison sited on the northern bank of the James River on the eastern fringe of the city.

"I say we crash out and take our chances," a voice growled in the pitch blackness of the windowless carriage, just loud enough to be heard above the clatter of slowing hooves and rumble of braking wheels on a cobbled surface.

"I'm with you all the way, Frank."

"Captain? If anyone goes out fast the Rebs'll likely blast all of us!"

In the four years since he had first fired a shot in this war, Hedges had been moulded from a shy, almost gentle farm boy into a vicious killer. And almost every minute of every day and night in that time he had been in the company of the six men who now shared the prison wagon with him. He didn't have to see the men, or even know where they were positioned in the cramped confinement to recognise who was speaking.

Sergeant Frank Forrest had made the crashout suggestion. The oldest man in the group, he was a mean-faced, mean-tempered man who had been a bounty hunter in the south-western territories and Mexico before the war. But he was also a good non-com—when he respected his commanding officer. And to earn the respect of Forrest a man had to prove himself smarter, tougher, meaner and a more cold-blooded killer than he was himself. So far, quick to learn the deadly lessons of a dirty war, the farm boy from Iowa had always come out on top in the run-ins with the professional murderer. Thus, because of this, Hedges had retained his tenuous authority over the whole bunch. For the other five, resigned to their lot of followers rather than leaders, had made it plain they would be as happy to take orders from Forrest instead of Hedges if that was the way the breaks went.

In this instance, it was Billy Seward who had voiced his

support for the sergeant's plan. He was a fresh-faced country boy who had come to enjoy war when he discovered within himself an insatiable lust to kill for the pure enjoyment of the act.

Bob Rhett was the inevitable objector: a tall, thin, weakly handsome New Englander from Boston who had proved his cowardice on countless occasions. He was never in favour of any move that was in the least part dangerous. Unless, perhaps, the reward offered an opportunity to indulge his homosexuality.

As the prison wagon came to a halt, the springs creaking and the team snorting, Hedges sensed the other three men awaiting his reaction to the plan. Hal Douglas, possibly the most incompetent corporal in the Union Army, who had been given his chevrons simply because he could read and write. And Roger Bell and John Scott, both troopers. All three of them ideal soldiers to fight this kind of war, whether the action be a full-scale battle like Bull Run, Shiloh, Lookout Mountain and Missionary Ridge or the behind-the-lines guerilla operations they had been forced to take part in during their escape from Andersonville.'* Not so coldly professional as Forrest or as hysterically homicidal as Seward, but nonetheless prepared to kill and to destroy with wanton disregard for everything save their own skins. Because Hedges had himself become detached from the broader issues of the war, he asked nothing more than this from his men who, discounting Rhett and assuming Forrest was prepared to stay in line, had been moulded into an almost perfect fighting unit.

The six-man army guard jumped down from the wagon and more footfalls rang against the cobbles as prison guards ran from the surrounding buildings. A heavy gate was slammed closed.

"Well, Captain?" Scott urged.

"I'm fine, trooper," Hedges replied evenly. "Might stay healthy at least until sun up if a bunch of crazy guys with the shit scared out of them don't get me killed right now."

Forrest uttered an angry grunt.

"You know somethin' we don't, sir?" Bell asked in a whisper as an eerie silence shrouded the wagon and its surroundings.

**See—Edge: Seven Out Of Hell.*

"Not a damn thing and I ain't ready to move until I know more than that."

"Makes sense!" Rhett hissed anxiously.

"Ass kisser from way back," Forrest growled.

Seward giggled. "Only direction to do it from."

"You men in there? You lousy spies!"

From the sharpness of the tone and the way in which the voice picked up a hint of an echo, Hedges guessed the wagon had been halted between high stone walls.

"We hear you, Reb!" Forrest yelled.

Hedges became tense, leaning forward from the bench seat, his muscles knotting for a dive to the wagon bed. From Forrest's tone of voice, he guessed the sergeant was not yet fully committed to a crash-out. But he wasn't prepared to trust the man's impulses. Hedges' own voice was little more than a hissed vibration in the stale air, fetid with the odours of bad breath and the unwashed body stink of sweating tension and fear.

"Any man not ready to die, hit the floor."

"The door's gonna be opened!" the voice shouted from outside the wagon. "Just one man even looks like giving trouble, you're all cold meat."

Two pairs of heels clattered on the cobbles, approaching the rear of the wagon. Keys scraped in padlocks, chains rattled and bolts screeched in their brackets.

"Why's the captain always so goddamn right, Frank?" Seward whined softly.

"Told you before, Billy," the sergeant muttered sourly. "Cause he knows that as soon as he calls a wrong shot, he's in the firin' line."

Relieved that he was not to face a hail of bullets, Rhett's spirits had risen. "Makes it a matter of life and death for Mr. Hedges," he said with a hollow laugh.

The door folded open and the Union troopers in a motley array of civilian garb blinked against the comparative brightness of the steadily burning oil lamps. As their eyes adjusted to the light level their other senses were heightened. They felt the dampness and chill of the early morning mist cooling the sweat on their flesh. They smelled the tangy dankness of the nearby river. And they heard the steady trickling of running water.

"Ain't none of us got the choice no more," Bell growled miserably as he surveyed the view from the wagon. "All gonna get it in the neck."

"Out slowly, one at a time, men on my right first."

The order made Hedges the first man to step from the wagon and he complied to the letter, easing up from the hard bench, stretching taut muscles and slouching down the two steps on to the damp cobbles. But the nonchalant obedience was a paper-thin protective shell. Just beneath the surface he was physically poised and mentally alert to lunge into lightning action if the opportunity was presented. But the clear blue eyes flashing from side to side beneath the hooded lids saw no such chance.

The wagon was halted at the centre of a large courtyard. It had not been turned after entering the prison so that, as the troopers emerged from the wagon, they saw the thirty foot high front wall with a pair of large double gates at a central point. A railed catwalk ran along the inside of the wall, six feet from the top. There was a wooden cabin at each corner and a larger one overlooking the gates. Lamps burned in each and spilled light through the slitted gunports, to glint on the rifle barrels angled down towards the wagon.

Fifteen more Spencer rifles covered the disembarking prisoners. Ten were trained upon them by a line of drab-brown uniformed prison guards positioned midway between the wagon and the gate. Five were aimed from the shoulders of the military escort aligned at one side. The lieutenant and the prison governor stood at the other side, showing no weapons.

"He sure in hell was right this time," Hal Douglas muttered as he took his place at the end of the line of prisoners and raked his frightened eyes over the grim faces of the riflemen. Then he craned around to look at the high front wall and the towering cell blocks enclosing the courtyard at the sides and rear.

"No talking!" the dour-faced sergeant at the head of the line of Rebel soldiers snapped as the lieutenant handed the execution warrants to the governor.

"Up your ass, Reb!" Forrest snarled at him. "We're signed and sealed to die anyhow. You figure to leather our butts before we swing if we ain't good boys?"

The grey-uniformed sergeant scowled.

"Talk about somethin' else, Frank," Billy Seward urged with a broad grin. "Bob's gettin' all stirred up. You know how he feels about asses and butts and stuff like that."

"No, Billy," Forrest drawled. "I don't know how he feels. I ain't never let him get that close to me."

Scott and Bell laughed.

Hedges, Rhett and Douglas ingored the mixture of bravado and hollow-humoured reaction to the seemingly hopeless plight in which the men found themselves. The New Englander and the corporal continued to survey their surroundings with gaunt eyes. Hedges retained his veneer of easy acceptance while he completed a detailed examination of the prison. In addition to the lamps in the guard cabins, other shafts of light sprang from windows here and there in the cell blocks. The moon was masked by the white mist blanketing the night sky but there was ample light to show that the courtyard offered no means of escape. Even when the military escort had been withdrawn and the line of prison guards dispersed, the men in the catwalk cabins would not be the only ones watching the courtyard. For other riflemen—two at each side and four at the rear—patrolled the flat roofs of the cell blocks: dark, spectre-like silhouettes against the pale vapour rolling across the prison from the river.

"Okay, you murderin' bastards. The soldier-boy's give me the papers so you all belong to me now." The governor glowered at the loose-knit, lounging group of prisoners. He was a big man, barrel-chested, bulging gutted and with a squarish head from which his dark eyes looked out with a cruel glint. He was about fifty.

"Richard Lovelace was out of his tiny mind," Rhett muttered after completing a final fearful-eyed survey of his surroundings.

"Told you, Frank," Seward reminded lightly. "All that ass talk's made Bob feverish."

"Get a medic," Forrest taunted the Rebel sergeant. "Our buddy's come over queer."

The Rebel seemed about to spit, but checked it. "Hope it ain't nothin' fatal," he rasped. "I wanna see him hang."

"Cheer up, Bob," Forrest said, beaming at the lanky New Englander. "Could be a gay night after all. Guy here wants to see the way you hang."

"Go to hell!" Rhett snarled at Forrest.

"He will," the sergeant said, with a grin of his own, "In good company."

"That man!" the governor roared. He thrust forward a rock-steady arm, the index finger pointing at Rhett. "Come here!"

"Who, me?" Rhett asked tremulously.

At a nod from the lieutenant, the soldiers ported their arms, then swung to the side and moved to the front of the wagon.

"Who the hell do you think I mean when I'm pointing at you?" the governor bellowed.

The soldiers climbed hurriedly up on to the wagon, as if anxious to get away from the dank-smelling prison.

"Captain?" Rhett pleaded shrilly.

"No doubt about it," Hedges told him evenly. "The man definitely wants you."

The wagon jerked forward and was steered in a tight turn, the open rear door flapping and banging. A prison guard moved out of the shadows at the foot of the high wall. Rhett inched forward nervously as the guard swung wide the big gates. The wagon rolled through on to the street and the gates swung shut. There was an awesome finality about the sound of them closing together. Rhett halted three feet in front of the governor and the big, ugly man lowered his arm to his side.

"One of them soldier boys said no noise," the governor said to Rhett. "Reason he ain't no higher than a sergeant is that he can maybe give orders, but he ain't so hot at seein' them carried out."

"Weren't only me," Rhett whined, shooting a terrified glance over his shoulder.

The knot of prisoners, exposed in the centre of the courtyard without the solid bulk of the wagon behind them, were somehow reduced in stature by the large expanse of cobblestones around them and the towering walls which trapped them. They looked as helplessly vulnerable as they were. And their expressions, ranging from fearful to blank, told Rhett he was the most pathetically situated of them all. Alone and not about to receive support. The sweat of terror dripped from Rhett's forehead into his eyes. But he was too frightened to move to rub away the stinging moisture.

"I'm a governor," the big, mean-faced man went on, his tone almost conversational now. "Top hand inside these walls. Got to be that by makin' damn sure orders were obeyed."

Rhett was trembling with fear. The other prisoner's saw his hands were clutched together behind his back. But, even locked thus, they shook uncontrollably.

"Not just my own orders, you understand. In my prison, anyone in authority—and that means anyone who ain't a prisoner—gets his orders obeyed. Okay?"

Rhett tried to speak, but the words got caught in his fear-constructed throat. He pumped his head several times. The governor shook his.

"I don't reckon you do, Yankee. Need a lesson. You won't be alive to remember it for much, so I'll keep it short."

As he spoke, he took a step forward, his right hand swinging upwards again. But there was no pointing finger this time. All the fingers were curled to form a claw—which sank a vicious hold on to Rhett's thin shoulder. The New Englander's cry of alarm emerged as a gurgle. Then the governor raised his left arm and began to slap Rhett across the cheeks. Palm and back of the hand. Not hard. Just enough to erupt a sharp crack at each contact. But the mild beating was designed only as a diversion to hold Rhett's humiliated attention. The real damage was done by the governor's left knee. He snapped it up hard and fast and jerked Rhett closer to him at the same moment. The kneecap slammed into the victim's groin and this time there was no obstacle to the scream. White hot agony swamped fear and

Rhett's airways were burst wide open to broadcast the high, thin shrillness that exploded inside him.

Instinctively, his body tried to fold, but the grip on his shoulder held him upright. The slapping stopped and the hand was withdrawn and bunched into a fist. The fist shot forward and the scream was curtailed. The grip on Rhett's shoulder was released and he staggered backwards, hands flying up from his lower stomach to clasp at this throat. Gagging from the blow to his windpipe, Rhett tripped over his own feet and fell hard to the cobbles in front of the other Union troopers. Fighting for breath, his body writhed, with legs flailing, as if to keep himself from drowning in the waves of pain washing over him.

The governor eyed the other prisoners, licking his lips with relish and not speaking until the dry retching sounds from Rhett's tortured throat had subsided to pitiful whimpers. Then. "School don't have to be out if any of you other Yankees want to do some learnin'."

From the corner of his eye, Hedges saw that Seward's mouth was opening to form the first word of an embittered retort. He took a step forward, to crouch down beside the pain-wracked form of Rhett. As he did so, he sank the heel of a boot hard on to Seward's toecap. The youngster yelled in pain.

"One cripple's more than enough to carry out of here," the Captain rasped from the side of his mouth.

"No takers?" the governor snapped, then gave a harsh laugh. "So pick up that heap of garbage and let's move."

"You figure there's a way outta here, Captain?" Forrest muttered as he helped to load Rhett's limp form on to Hedges' shoulder. "Heard what you told Billy."

"We cracked Andersonville," Hedges reminded softly.*

"Piece of cake compared to this rockpile." Forrest growled, glancing around grimly at the high stone walls enclosing them.

"Different kind of cake is all," Hedges murmured and raised a hand to touch the back of his neck beneath the long hair. "Needs to be sliced a different way."

Forrest showed the trace of an evil grin as he recognised the

**See—Edge: The Blue, The Grey And The Red.*

action: a sign that when they were searched the concealed razor had been overlooked.

"Right, the doorway in the rear corner!" the governor barked. "Move it."

He went to the head of the column and the guards flanked the prisoners as they shuffled forward across the cobblestones. Forrest was the last man in the line with Hedges in front of him, rigidly upright in his gait despite the burden of Rhett. The New Englander groaned, surfacing from his unconsciousness.

"Go to sleep again, you stupid bastard," Forrest muttered. "We were talkin' about rock cake. Not friggin' fruit cake."

HEADING into the wind-driven rain, Luke held down the pace on the return to Paradise. The men talked sporadically, prefixing each given name with the title "angel". Luke was the only one referred to as "arch angel".

Riding at the rear of the twin column, right hand palmed over the butt of the holstered Colt, Edge soon gave up trying to overhear what was said. Against the howl of the wind and hiss of the rain, counterpointed by the rushing sounds of the stream, he could not discern enough isolated words to make sense of the desultory conversations.

Beyond the mouth of the gorge, the wind veered and swirled so that the rain was not constantly hurled into the faces of the riders. Visibility lengthened and was reduced by turns as the teeming downpour swirled and billowed like some enormous grey curtain.

"You guys can certainly pray up a storm," the half-breed yelled as he held on his hat against the violent tug of the wind. "Any chance of getting through the word for a let-up?"

"Do not mock us." The speaker was a gaunt-faced man named Angel Angus who rode immediately ahead of Edge at the rear of the left hand file. His voice was thick with a Scottish accent unmarred by American drawl. He turned in the saddle to glare back at Edge. "The sky was bright when we gave the sinners unto the mercy of the Lord."

"For doing what?" the half-breed asked, his hooded eyes glancing swiftly from left to right. To the east the stream had widened to fifty feet, rushing forward with a frenetic energy, muddy brown along a depth that was impossible to gauge. On the western slope of the valley, the trees grew thick and impenetrable, spreading down on to level ground.

"The two sinners you freed were found guilty of making obscene suggestions to female angels," Angus replied. "The sinner Patrick O'Rerry was condemned for laying lascivious hands upon the same females."

"The sinners were mindless with the Devil's brew," a stocky, acne-skinned man named Angel Francis augmented earnestly. "Foul-tongued and reeling. Such men have never entered Paradise before."

"Hell's just got be overcrowded," Edge said coolly.

Francis chose to ignore the half-breed's wry comment. "Arch Angel Luke was adamant the sinner O'Rerry should perish from execution rock," he went on. "But he was unsure how to punish the other two. In his wisdom, he sought the counsel of the Lord. We prayed and the rains came."

"And the Devil's agent interrupted the work of the Lord," Angus thundered. "Prophet Thomas had a vision that mischief was afoot. That is why we rode hard for the gorge."

Edge was not listening to the broad and oddly flat rantings of the Scotsman. The storm was slackening, the wind dropping then stopping altogether so that the rain pelted straight down for a while. Then, overhead, the clouds began to roll rather than scud and the dark streaks were whisped away to leave the sky higher, lighter and drier. The whole valley came into long, wide view. Ahead it was bending towards the north-west and broadening, the river following the line of least resistance along its centre. Then, as the group of riders completed the dog-leg turn, the rain stopped altogether and the town of Paradise came into view.

It was perched on a shallow slope a little way up the valley side, and from a distance looked much like any other small community in the timberland of the north-western territories. But, as Luke quickened the pace to a canter and the riders drew nearer, the half-breed was able to see the neat simplicity of the cluster of buildings. All of them were stoutly built of logs from the timber cleared from the site of the town. A single street ran up the slope and at the lower end was flanked by two long buildings. One was a barn and the other a stable block. The houses, which were little more than shacks only big enough to contain two rooms, were aligned at the sides of the street on higher ground, every one identical to its neighbour. Every building was single storey.

Spread out on the valley floor below the town was a wide area of productive land stretching to a construction site on the bank of the river. Fields of sprouting wheat, barley, potatoes and green vegetables exuded freshness after the rain storm. Beyond this patchwork of fields was a wide swathe of verdant pastureland, fenced to keep a herd of Texas Longhorns off the growing crops.

To a man with more imagination than Edge—less of a realist—the fact that the sun suddenly shafted through a break in the cloud to bathe the town and farmland with bright yellow light . . . such an occurence might have appeared as a physical manifestation of heaven's alliance with the Earthly Angels. But the half-breed merely sighed with relief as the cloud-break widened and the warmth of the sun's rays reached him and began to dry his clothing.

"Is it not a beautiful place to die?" Angus proclaimed earnestly as the pace slackened to a walk and the riders began moving along a pebble-surfaced trail between the fields.

"No place is that if a man ain't ready," Edge muttered as he looked across the construction site which was the starting point of the trail. It was an area some five hundred feet by a hundred, covered with newly spread cement and enclosed by a stone wall of irregular height—no more than ten feet tall at its highest point. There was a wide gap at the north end.

"The start of the Cathedral of Paradise!" Angus announced with pride. "When it is completed it will be the most magnificent House of the Lord in the New world."

"If we live long enough to finish the work," Francis responded miserably.

"It will be finished!" the Scotsman said vehemently.

As the riders came off the valley floor and Luke called a halt outside the stable block, the doors of the small, crudely built shacks opened and the other citizens of Paradise emerged into the new sunlight. They advanced just a few feet into the street and stood, waiting. Every man was dressed exactly like those who had ridden to the gorge. And the women were just as sombrely attired, the skirts of their black dresses sweeping the ground and the stiff-collars thrusting high enough to prod their throats. Each wore a poke bonnet with every strand of hair tucked up inside.

They looked at Edge coolly, unprovoked by the impassive stare with which he responded to their appraisal. More than three-quarters of the eyes which examined him were weak with age, peering out from sockets surrounded by the wrinkled skin of long life. He saw only two women young enough to have attracted the fur-trappers: in their twenties and still showing traces of youthful prettiness. The remainder were all over fifty, he guessed. There were no children.

"Animals are not admitted into our town," Luke intoned, dismounting with careful dignity. "If you will wait here, sinner, an angel will come shortly to attend to the needs of your horse and yourself."

The other riders climbed from their saddles and Francis gathered up the reins and led the horses into the stables.

"My vision was right!" a squeaky voice called from the far end of the street.

Edge was gazing idly in that direction, towards a level area beyond the town at the foot of a towering wall of sheer rock face thrusting three hundred feet up to an overhang. Spread over this area was a set of stocks, a whipping post and a pillory. All were empty.

"This man saw fit to release the two sinners we gave unto the punishment of the Lord!" Luke announced, raking his eyes across the blank faces of the townspeople.

A midget of a man—no more than five feet tall, with silver hair and a round face with a button nose and shiny, coal black eyes—stepped forward from the crowd at the far end of the street. "There was mischief!" he said shrilly. "Did I not predict it?"

"Do not be proud, Prophet Thomas!" Luke boomed with a trace of anger. "Your powers are a gift of the Lord."

Many heads swung towards the little man and he faded fast back into the crowd, his face flushed with embarrassment. The men who had ridden out to the gorge with Luke now began to move sedately up the sloping street. Their fellow citizens waited for them to pass, then slowly followed them, forming a procession towards the punishment area at the top. Luke held back, and turned to look up at the still mounted half-breed.

"Our ways must appear strange to you, sinner," he said.

Edge took out the makings and began to roll a cigarette. "You hear me asking any questions, Luke?" he asked easily.

But the white-haired old man was determined to say his piece. "We Earthly Angels have come to this place to forsake all sin, to build an edifice to the glory of the Lord and to die."

The half-breed licked the gummed paper, the back of his hand rasping over the stubble on his jaw. "I ain't here to rock your boat, feller," he allowed. "Just to buy some feed and supplies and get my horse shod."

Luke was not ready to be swayed from his purpose. "We raise crops and cattle, eat a little ourselves and sell the bulk to raise money to build the edifice. We believe all events to be the will of the Lord."

Edge lit the cigarette and swung down from the saddle. "The Lord said point those Starrs at me, then he said lower them again." He leaned down to unfasten the saddle cinch.

At the other end of town, the black-clad citizenry were forming a circle around the punishment area.

"We cannot spare money for powder and shot," Luke replied evenly, and abruptly captured the interest of the half-breed. "It was the will of the Lord that you chose to threaten the Earthly Angel and thus evade capture. Just as it was the will of the Lord that the two sinners were set free." He turned and pointed up towards the overhang at the top of the towering cliff face. It was almost noon and both he and Edge had to squint against the glare of the high sun. "That is execution rock. We must see if it is the will of the Lord that the sinner Patrick O'Rerry lives or dies."

All the clouds had fled southwards now and the three men standing on top of the flat overhang of rock were skylined against a clear blue ceiling of infinity. Despite the distance, it was possible to see that two of the men were dressed in the familiar stovepipe hats and frock coats. The man between them wore a check shirt and blue levis. His arms were tied in the same manner as Gabb and Mackinlay.

"Guess betting ain't allowed in Paradise?" Edge muttered as he dropped his saddle in the stable entrance. "The odds are sure stacked high against that guy surviving."

He hitched the stallion to the doorpost and slid the Winchester from the saddleboot.

"The sinner O'Rerry laid his lustful hands upon the female Angels, Sarah and Edith," Luke intoned as he began to accompany Edge up the sloping street. "His crime was therefore more serious than that of the sinners Gabb and Mackinlay who made lewd suggestions. Among the gamut of sins we forsake as Earthly Angels is the fulfilment of carnal desires."

Edge realised, disinterestedly, that it explained the absence of children in Paradise. And why the man named Francis was concerned the cathedral would not be built before the ageing citizens were all dead.

"It is important you know the reasons for what we do," Luke said as they reached the end of the street and a break appeared in the circle to allow them to join it. "We are not violent people. This is the first occasion we have found the need to utilise execution rock. Minor crimes are punished in the pillory, the stocks or at the whipping post. In an imperfect world such evils are necessary to dispense justice to the evil-doers."

"I foresee no escape for the sinner!" Prophet Thomas proclaimed in his squeaky voice. "It is the will of the Lord that he shall perish!"

Edge canted the rifle across his shoulder and hung the cigarett at the corner of his thin mouth. He squinted up the face of the cliff to where the helpless prisoner had been nudged to the lip of the overhang. "The little guy don't believe in tipping longshots, does he?" he muttered.

"The Lord's will be done!" Luke boomed, raised his hand, then dropped it abruptly.

The circle of black-garbed religious maniacs turned their blank faces towards the sunlit sky and clasped their hands together in prayer. Not a sound was uttered. The two executioners gave the condemned man a final push in the back. He toppled forward with his body held rigid, like a felled tree. But then, as he sensed the yawning space beneath him, he struggled against the free fall. His bound knees thudded up against his chest and he snapped his head from side to side. He turned over and over like an irregularly shaped ball, his arms lashed firmly to his sides. Edge was curious about the man's eerie silence, until he straightened his body and began to twist. Then the half-breed saw the tight gag covering the mouth.

The man hit the hard-packed ground in front of the stocks, full-stretch and head-first. There was a hiss of displaced air, then an awesome crunch as his skull impacted. The scalp split and then the bone splintered into a million fragments. The head exploded in a shower of spraying blood, brain matter, torn flesh and gleaming bone shards. The dead body slammed into a fold, the abdomen crashing down over the top of the stocks. The skin burst and the gory mess of the intestines spewed out, wrenching the balloon-like stomach free of the flesh. The sound was that of a splash, followed by the sharp crack of the breaking spine. The two halves of the broken body splattered to the ground at either side of the stocks.

"The will of the Lord has been done!" Luke announced into the solid silence which followed the ghastly noise of the crashing death.

"It is as I predicted, Angels of Paradise!" the tiny Prophet Thomas responded.

His voice shook with excitement and it was the only sign of emotion around the circle. The eyes of all the other sombrely-dressed townspeople looked at the suddenly fly-covered halves of the dead man with utter lack of expression.

"His mouth was covered to halt the blasphemous protestations issuing from it," Luke explained to the half-breed.

Edge sucked a final lungful of smoke from the cigarette, then dropped it and ground out the red ash beneath his heel as he looked up at execution rock. Then his hooded eyes followed the course taken by the falling body and settled on the mutilated remains where the flies fed. "Guess he was mad at being the fall guy," he said wryly. "Sure is a long way to tip O'Rerry."

CHAPTER THREE

THE cell was on the ground floor of the rear block, through an iron door with a Judas hole bored in it. It was about twelve feet square with a small barred, glassless window high up close to the ceiling ten feet overhead. The walls were of mortared blocks of stone, the ceiling of stout boarding and the floor of cracked and broken concrete. It smelled of damp and rot and human waste. It contained no bunks or chairs. It did have two prisoners already.

Enough silvered moonlight trickled through the high window to show the two bearded, filthy, ragged dressed men cowering in a corner as the governor flung open the door and Spencer muzzles urged the newcomers inside.

"Company for you two yellow-belly deserters!" the governor yelled gleefully as he slammed the door closed. "Don't trouble with anything special. Won't be with you long. Big trip tomorrow. Got to make an early start."

"Ain't he a funny man!" Scott growled miserably as Hedges dropped Rhett ungently to the floor.

"A barrel of friggin' laughs," one of the bearded men muttered.

"We get to splittin' our sides just thinkin' what the bastard's gonna do next," the other man augmented.

They both had the drawling voices which told of a Deep South background.

"Guess it makes life here bearable?" Bell sighed, sinking to the floor, his back against a damp-run wall.

Rhett lay where he had fallen, groaning his pain. The other troopers followed Bell's example.

"Billy, give me a boost to that window!" Hedges snapped after his eyes had adjusted to the low light level and he had made a survey of the cell.

Seward grimaced. "Frank?"

"Yeah?" the sergeant answered.

"We still takin' orders from the Captain?"

Forrest was resting his back against the iron door. Across from him was a latrine hole scooped out of the broken concrete and the earth beneath. It was from here that the cell's most noxious odour rose. He rolled some spit around in his mouth with a moist sound and then streaked it across the floor and into the latrine. "You got an idea how to get us out of this stinkin' joint, trooper?" he asked.

"Army don't pay me to think up ideas," Seward answered sourly.

"So do like Mr Hedges tells you and pray he can earn what Uncle Sam pays *him*."

Scowling, Seward moved close to the wall below the window and arched his back, bracing himself with his hands gripped around his knees. "Just glad Bob ain't a Captain," he muttered as Hedges climbed up on to his back and stood erect.

"Don't kid yourself!" the New Englander rasped through gritted teeth. "You bend down in front of me all you'd get up your ass is a foot."

"Friggin' boastin' again!" Douglas said with a hollow laugh.

It was the only expression of amusement. The other troopers glanced disconsolately around the cell and took their mood of misery from the fact that there was apparently no way out. Standing at his full height on Seward's straining back, Hedges had already decided upon the way of escape. But before starting the men to work he wanted to see what awaited them immediately outside. He surveyed the scene through narrowed, thoughtful eyes, his lean features betraying no hint of his reactions.

Beyond the window was a long compound, fenced at either end, with the James River forming the boundary opposite the prison's rear cell block. Across the slow-moving, moon-silvered water was the dark, sleeping city of Richmond, its skyline dominated by church steeples and towers. As Hedges raked his gaze over the dark mass of the city, relieved at intervals by the occasional illuminated window, a clock struck the hour of two. The notes had the mournful sound of a short death knell. But this idea was triggered by the scene in the compound immediately below the window.

Fourteen unarmed guards were at work, using picks and shovels to scoop out seven graves across the centre of the compound. At sunrise, the graves would be in direct line to be darkly barred by the shadow from the vertical strut of the platform gallows which stood ominously at the eastern side of the compound. They worked two men to a grave in the damp, misty night: digging and scooping with smooth speed: aware of the dawn deadline they had to meet.

"You gonna stay up there stargazing the whole damn night?" Seward groaned. "My back's damn near breakin'."

"Then it must be as weak as your lousy brain!" Forrest snarled. "Billy, you stay there and keep your mouth buttoned until Mr Hedges is good and ready to come down."

Hedges allowed a trace of a smile to turn up the corners of his mouth now. Forrest's attitude to the man was a sure barometer to his usefulness as a non-com: an indication of whether or not he felt able to handle any given situation. In these circumstances, it was obvious he would have no alternatives to the orders Hedges intended to give.

"I've seen enough, sergeant," the Captain announced, and dropped to the floor.

Seward straightened up, groaning and massaging the small of his back.

"Captain . . . sergeant?" one of the bearded men muttered thoughtfully. "Hey, you guys ducked outta the army, too?"

"Shut up, Floyd!" the other long-term prisoner warned.

The Union troopers, who had tilted their heads to listen to Hedges, abruptly swung to glare at the strangers.

"We look like yellow-bellies?" Scott snarled, then shrugged. "Apart from Bob, of course."

Floyd responded to the belligerent glares with a scowl. The other man looked scared, huddling closer to the wall.

"We ain't at our best right now," Forrest growled. "When we are, we're the best friggin' fightin' unit in the Union army, you crumbs!"

Floyd's anger rose. "Union? Friggin' Yankees! You didn't oughta be here in Riverside! Regular camp for captured Feds is over on Belle Isle!" He turned to the trembling prisoner whose fear heightened with every word spoken. "Ain't that so, Myron? It ain't right we gotta share quarters with a bunch of no-good Yankees."

While the man was looking at him so intently, Myron became fearfully fascinated by the mean face of Frank Forrest. What we saw caused him to try to motion Floyd into silence. But the shrieking man was too incensed to pay heed.

"Don't hurt my brother, mister!" Myron implored in a croaking voice. "We been locked up here since Fair Oaks. Almost two years. It's been too much for him. He's stir crazy!"

"I ain't sharin' my quarters with no Northern shitheads!" Floyd yelled. He sprang to his feet and lunged for the door, beating against it with his fists.

Forrest plunged into a private world of rage of his own, his mind closed to outside influences. He rose, whirled and fastened an iron-handed grip on Floyd's beard. Then, with a vicious wrench, he yanked the man away from the door and slammed him to the floor. The Union troopers cheered and whistled in encouragement, drowning Floyd's cry of pain and alarm. Myron was too frightened to move. Hedges leaned his back against the wall, the impassive, lean features not revealing his train of thought: which was concerned with the fact that the incident had snapped his men out of their depression.

Forrest, his weathered, time-beaten face set in the lines of an evil grin of pleasure, hauled Floyd from one side of the cell to the other then flipped him over on to his belly. He released his hold on the man's beard, straightened up and thudded a boot down hard on to the back of the helpless man's neck. Floyd's cries of protest were muffled as his head was forced down the putrid-smelling latrine hole. Then, as the evil miasma infiltrated his nostrils, Floyd began to vomit. With each moist retch and wet splash, his dimished strength was reduced further and soon his emaciated body ceased to struggle.

"We're so damn good, Johnnie Rebs just get sick with fear from lookin' at us," the grinning sergeant proclaimed. Then he removed his heel from Floyd's neck, crouched and jerked up the man's head by grabbing a handful of his hair. "Right, crumb?"

Floyd's face was drained of colour beneath the ingrained dirt. But his eyes blazed with the power of hate. "I never feel fine when I see and smell a load of crap!" he taunted.

"Please?" Myron managed to croak into the solid, tension-brittle silence that followed Floyd's insult. "My brother don't know what he's saying, mister."

"Don't stand for that, sarge!" Billy Seward yelled.

"Kill the bastard, Frank!" Bob Rhett shrieked.

Forrest's anger had changed from hot, through evil humour, to ice cold. In this state, he was able to react to suggestions not triggered in his own mind. Hedges saw this and knew the man was ready to follow Rhett's urging.

"We need all the help we can get to bust out of here, sergeant," the Captain said softly. "But it don't have to smell sweet."

Forrest nodded his understanding and grinned his appreciation of the idea. Once more he changed his grip from a hand to a foot hold on Floyd. There was nothing left in the man's stomach to vacate into the hole. His retching was painfully dry. Then Forrest stooped, gripped Floyd's ankles, up-ended him and dropped him head-first into the latrine hole.

"Now who's a shithead, Reb?" Forrest demanded against the nauseating sounds of Floyd fighting for breath through the stinking slime at the bottom of the hole.

He flung the kicking legs away from him and Myron scuttled across the cell to rescue his brother from drowning.

"Okay, Captain, how we gonna bust out of here?" Forrest asked, rubbing his hands together, enjoying the final few moments of pleasure.

Hedges moved over close to the outside wall of the cell and crouched down. He inserted his long, brown fingers into a wide crack in the concrete and levered up a slab to expose the earth beneath. "You set the yellow-belly Reb on the right course," he told Forrest, then showed a cold grin to the confused troopers. "But I'm a bit more particular about the kind of hole I crawl into."

It was the latrine that had given Hedges the idea for tunnelling out of the cell: that and the general state of disrepair of the floor.

"I ain't no friggin' mole," Seward rasped.

"And I can't do no digging after getting a kick in the balls like that," Rhett complained.

"Sergeant?" Hedges asked, and all the men looked at the sour-faced non-com.

Forrest spat. "It ain't gonna be like slicin' no cake, sir," he growled.

"Something you all ought to see," Hedges invited, and went to the wall, circling around the crouching Myron who was trying to clean the mess from his brother's hair and beard. He stooped down in the same manner as Seward had done earlier. "Take a look. And no cracks about Rhett. There isn't time. There isn't time for anything except digging."

One at a time, the men climbed on to his back and peered out at the scene of the gallows and the seven graves in process of being dug. Forrest was the last man to sink his boot heels in Hedges' back and see the physical evidence of the threat which hung over them. When he stepped down, he spat again and raked abruptly glinting eyes over the nervous faces.

"Billy ain't no mole, and neither are any of us. But one way or another we gonna go underground. Reckon Captain Hedges' way is the best.

"Rebs gonna help?" Hal Douglas wanted to know.

"What do you think?" Forrest asked, glaring at the bearded brothers.

"I reckon they're gonna help," Roger Bell supplied.

It was muscle-aching, energy-draining, sweat-pouring work in the evil smelling cell which was almost airless but for the meagre trickle which infiltrated the tiny barred window. And grimly slow, for seven prisoners had to squat idly by while two at a time scratched out the tunnel with fragments of concrete and their bare hands. For Floyd and Myron it was nauseating, too. For, urged by the menace in Forrest's glinting eyes, they had chosen to work together in a team and there was no way to clean all the human excrement from Floyd's beard and hair: and in a three-feet-square tunnel the air soon grew thick with the overpowering stench of the man.

The shaft had to be sunk four feet deep to reach below the foundation of the wall before the tunnel proper could start. Initially, the two men who were working cursed the earth and each other, applying their energy but not their hearts to the task. But, as their strength ebbed seemingly in direct relation to the inch-by-inch progress made, the bitter words ceased. They worked with one man clawing and scraping at the earth and the other stretched on the floor on his belly, scooping out the displaced soil. The heap against the wall grew gradually larger and after awhile it was high enough for those men who were resting to stand on it and peer through the window.

The seven graves had been dug now and the compound was deserted. The sight of the ominous pits with the evil shape of the gallows nearby inevitably drove the men to work more furiously in the lengthening tunnel. The placid peace of the scene beyond the window, marred only by the quiet sounds of the river, the subdued throb of the sleeping city and the chiming of the distant clock, seemed to enhance the fearful eeriness.

"Somethin's been botherin' me, Bob," Forrest said wearily against the ringing chimes sounding the hour of five o'clock.

Hedges was at the window and he turned to look down into the cell, suddenly aware he could see the men much more clearly than before. Their dirt-heavy clothing, their grimed and sweat-run faces and their bruised and bloodied hands. He had been so intent upon studying the world outside for signs of activity, he had failed to notice the sky lightening towards dawn.

The sergeant was being helped out of the hole by the New Englander who was his working partner.

"What's that sarge?" The lines of pain and exhaustion were etched deeply into the weak handsomeness of Rhett's face.

Forrest was approaching the same degree of exhaustion, but

he managed to show his tobacco-stained teeth and back the grin with a glint in his eyes. "Who the hell's this guy Lovelace you figure to be nuts?"

Seward and Scott rose from squatting against the wall and shuffled towards the hole. Rhett's hollow-eyed, sunken-cheeked face became creased by a frown as he searched his jaded mind.

"Out in the courtyard awhile back," Hedges recalled for the lanky fag, and curled his lips to show a grin of his own as he sensed the genuineness of Forest's good humour.

Rhett sank to the floor and rubbed his eyes. "He was a poet. British. Seventeenth century!' He yawned.

"Nice we ain't gonna die ignorant," John Scott rasped scornfully.

"Wrote something like: 'Stone walls do not a prison make, nor iron bars a cage'," Rhett quoted wearily.

"Wasn't just nuts," Roger Bell groaned. "He was a friggin' ravin' lunatic."

"Not if he was thinkin' about guys like us," Forrest answered, stretching out full-length on the floor. "I reckon we're under the rock and can start goin' up."

There was a stretched second of utter silence inside the cell. Every man caught his breath and stared into Forrest's relaxing face with incredulous awe. Then the first grey light of dawn struck the bared teeth of each Union trooper.

"Yell and you'll hang!" Hedges rasped to fill the silence a moment before the wild sounds of unleashed excitement could shatter it. "Get down the hole, Billy. And no goofing off."

"Captain's right," Forrest said urgently, his exhaustion falling from him like a garment he had shed as he sat up. "Guards hear party sounds from the death cell they ain't gonna just think we're happy to be outta the war."

It was as if the frustration of being unable to vent their joy was channelled through an emotional-physical reversal to emerge as a burst of renewed energy desperate for release. Douglas and Bell could hardly wait for Seward and Scott to finish their stint in the tunnel. Then Floyd and Myron went to work with a will they had not shown before. Forrest and Rhett replaced the Rebel deserters. Nobody wanted Hedges to spell him and the Captain remained at the window, his impassive ice-blue eyes showing no sign of the anxiety he felt as the sky above the sleeping city grew greyer by the minute.

The compound remained empty, except for a lark which settled on the uppermost cross-strut of the gallows and began to signal the start of the dawn chorus. The far-off clock scared the bird into flight with the chimes of five-thirty. Hedges became aware that, until now, the note of the bell had possessed the quality of a death-knell. But, as the final clang faded into the misty morning, he heard it as an alarm. A crack appeared in the trampled ground three feet to the left of the window, two feet from the wall. Then the fingers of a hand clawed up through the crack. They flexed, as if testing the feel of free, clean air.

Hedges experienced a stab of elation. Almost as powerful as the surge of exhilaration that possessed him at the outset of every battle, swamping his true nature so that he could kill and maim and destroy with all the impunity to conscience of the killer that war had made of him. But in the next instant an ice-cold calm swept over him. A picket gate in the compound's perimeter fence had opened.

"Hold it!" he snapped over his shoulder. He heard the order repeated along the tunnel. Then he returned his hooded-eyed gaze to the gate.

The bulky figure of the prison governor stepped into the compound. Carefully, the big man closed and latched the gate behind him. For a few moments, he surveyed the enclosed area, then he took a cigar from under his coat and lit it. The fingers withdrew into the crack, like the feelers of some bizarre insect which had sensed danger. The governor began to stroll across the compound. Hedges reached a hand under the long hair at the nape of his neck and drew the razor from its pouch. He tossed the weapon down to Seward who was crouched at the side of the hole.

"One man," he said. "I'll say when. Then a count of five before a show."

Again the order was passed along the tunnel. This time, the

razor accompanied it. Floyd and Myron sat huddled in a corner, unable to comprehend the cryptic words which were instantly understood by the troopers: amazed by the coolness of the Union men as they waited in the tense silence for the signal to action. But the Rebels had opted out of the war too early. Had no chance to become moulded into a cohesive group under battle conditions. Had not experienced situations in which individual personalities and enmities were subjugated by the need for common, rather than self, preservation. Had never known circumstances when split-second decisions had to be made and instant orders given and obeyed. Had not learned the harsh lessons of a vicious war.

The governor ambled over to the gallows and looked up at the suspended noose. He blew a smoke ring at it but the insubstantial circle of greyness disintegrated long before it reached the rope. Then, with the cigar clamped between his teeth and his hands clasped behind his back, the big man walked along the line of graves, glancing down into each and giving curt nods of satisfaction. Abruptly, he sensed watching eyes and his head snapped up. He looked in many directions before his dark eyes came to rest on the barred window of the cell with Hedges' face a pale blur beyond. His teeth became bared in a cruel grin around the tight-held cigar and he began to take long strides towards the rear wall of the prison block. He halted about three feet to the left of where a crack in the ground marked the tunnel's exit point.

"Looks like it's gonna be a nice mornin' for a hangin', soldier boy," he greeted expansively, snatching the cigar from his mouth and expelling smoke up towards Hedges. Its aromatic scent was a pleasant contrast to the fetid atmosphere filling the cell.

"The pleasure'll be all yours, feller," Hedges answered.

The governor shook his head. "Not mine alone, soldier boy. You ain't no ordinary spies. President intends to make a big event out of this necktie party. Comin' himself and bringin' along some guests. Whole bunch of soldier boys'll be here, too. Hear tell there's a chance General Robert E. Lee will be present."

"The best the South has got is nothing less than we deserve," Hedges said wryly.

"Course," the governor continued, unbuttoning his topcoat, then clamping the cigar back between his teeth as he worked on his pants' flies. "Means the show will start a little late. Got to take the fences down so we all get a good view of you guys doing the mid-air dance."

The governor groped into the front of his pants, then stepped closer to the wall to urinate.

"Not sunrise anymore?" Hedges asked in the same tone as before. Then, against the splash of water on the wall, his voice rose for the single word: "When?"

The word was hissed along the tunnel. Bell and Douglas used their initiative to guard against an eventuality. In unison, they crouched in front of the two Rebels and Floyd and Myron suddenly found filthy hands clamped across their mouths.

The governor laughed harshly around his cigar. "Don't worry none, soldier boy. You'll be one of the first to know when the show starts."

Hedges had a moment of worry when the man at the head of the tunnel burst through the cracked ground and was boosted out by the man behind him. It was Bob Rhett. But in the next instant he had peered through the dirt on the New Englander's face and recognised the expression it carried. He was scared, certainly—Rhett was constantly in a funk when he was close to the enemy. But he possessed the coward's natural bent for viciousness when the circumstances allowed. And they were good now. The governor had his back towards Rhett and both hands were busily engaged. Added to this was the fact that Rhett's victim was no ordinary unknown enemy. The governor had hurt him badly out in the courtyard. So hatred as well as kill-lust contorted the New Englander's thin features as he side-stepped and then moved forward.

"No last requests?" Hedges asked easily.

Rhett's timing had been good. He had waited the designated five seconds before breaking clear of the tunnel. He stayed cool, positioning himself perfectly for the kill.

"Ask for anythin' you like, soldier boy," the governor invited as he finished peeing. He looked up at the window, eyes glinting with scorn. "Course, you won't get a goddamn thing."

"You're a hard man, governor," Hedges rasped, holding his attention.

Rhett had the natural grace of the homosexual. Close to the governor, but not touching him—holding his breath to keep from releasing a warning stream of warm air against the thick neck—he rose on to his toes. He lifted both arms like a ballet dancer at the start of a routine. The fingers of his left hand were splayed and those of his right were clamped around the handle of the razor.

"Flattery won't earn you anythin', soldier boy," the governor rasped, and snatched the cigar from his mouth to bellow with laughter.

But he didn't have the time. Rhett arched his body forward and swung his arms inwards. Terror replaced humour in the governor's eyes. Rhett's left hand fastened over his mouth, the fingers snapping closed. The New Englander pivoted his body slightly to extend the length of his reach over the governor's right shoulder. Then the hand punched towards the left side of the victim's neck. The blade of the razor sank an inch into the soft flesh beneath the ear. Then it was ripped in a sideways arc. The governor's eyes bulged with alarm, then agony. A muffled grunt escaped Rhett's tightening hand. Blood sprayed from punctured skin, then gouted as the jugular vein was severed. A weary sigh followed the grunt and was the governor's dying sound. Rhett pulled the razor free below the right ear. He released the dead man and tipped him away with his elbows. The governor splashed his unfeeling face into the pool of his own urine. His blood was like dark smoke clouding the yellow liquid.

Rhett grinned proudly up at Hedges, reaching to hand back the razor. "Did I give that bastard what he deserved," the New Englander muttered as Forrest snaked out through the hole in the ground and eyed the governor's body with cold venom.

"He got what he came over for," Hedges answered as Seward put in an appearance out in the compound. "Wanted a slash."

Then he stepped down from the heap of earth and wiped the

blood from the razor before sliding it back into the pouch and going headfirst into the tunnel behind Bell.

The final traces of night had almost disappeared when Forrest and Douglas gripped him under the armpits and hauled him out of the hole on the other side of the wall. Rhett was searching the governor's body for weapons. He had to be content with a silver watch. Seward had located the discarded cigar and was drawing against it luxuriously. Bell and Scott were staring at the two Rebels with hard eyes more menacing than gun muzzles would have been. When the hooded gaze of Hedges swung towards them, Floyd and Myron stepped backwards as if driven by a physical force.

"I get an inkling you're gonna foul us up, you're dead," the Captain hissed. "Got it?"

Neither man trusted himself to speak. Both swallowed hard and nodded.

"Let's move," Hedges ordered, and set off at a trot. He recalled the last occasion he and his men had been behind enemy lines with unwanted company. It had worked out fine then: but those men had been freed slaves.*

The others fell in behind him in single file, Bell and Scott assuming responsibility for Floyd and Myron, staying close at the heels of the nervous brothers. Hedges led the men along the foot of the wall, then stayed close in to the fence to the water's edge. There they halted a moment, some casting tense glances up at the roof of the cell block, searching for the silhouettes of patrolling guards against the now distinctly grey sky of the new day. None showed.

Hedges eased his head forward to peer around the end of the fence, looking upstream. What he saw caused his lips to crack in a tight grin. A vacant lot spread with garbage rotting among scrub grass, then the high wall of a warehouse at the edge of a dock complex. Tied up at bow and stern alongside the wharf fronting the warehouse was a Rebel ironclad. The ship rose and fell almost imperceptibly. Nothing else moved on water or land.

**See—Edge: Vengeance is Black.*

"We're out, but a long way from home," Forrest muttered from immediately behind Hedges.

Freedom had fed the familiar sourness back into the sergeant's tone and Hedges noted there was no suffix of rank to the remark.

"I ain't through yet, *sergeant*," Hedges rasped.

"No, *sir*," came the response, with a hint of scorn and a grimace to reinforce the point. "What now?"

"River trip should be good for us after being cooped up—like chickens, some of us."

Forrest's eyes glinted dangerously at the taunt. But he was no longer in a panic situation. Merely perilous, and that was nothing new. He could control his anger and store it, along with his already generous supply, for future use.

Hedges moved down the bank and into the cold water of the James River. The men followed him. And saw the ship for the first time—grey-painted and ugly looking in the dawn light. The colours of the Confederacy hung limp and unmoving from a short mast at the bow.

Forrest spat and rubbed his punished hands together in keen anticipation as he entered the river.

"How about that, Bob?" Hal Douglas chided as the New Englander stepped tentatively into the chill water. "Maybe you'll get some naval action. You know what sailors are."

"Sonofabitch!" Rhett hissed as, like the others, he crouched low so that just his head remained above the surface.

"Don't get all steamed up at Hal," Seward muttered with a giggle.

"Maybe you'll get a chance to shoot some seamen," Bell whispered with a soft laugh. "Might even be able to raise a rear admiral!"

EDGE crouched in the shadow of the stable wall, listening to the sounds of Angel Francis shoeing the black stallion, and thinking about his dead wife*.

An hour had past since Patrick O'Rerry had paid the crushing

See—Edge: Sioux Uprising.

price for doing more than merely look at the only nubile women in the town of Paradise. Now, the execution might never have taken place. The shattered body had been buried in an unmarked grave and every last drop of spilled blood and spewed gore had been cleaned from the punishment area. After a morning wasted dealing with the so-called sinners, the sombrely dressed citizens of Paradise had hurried their spartan midday meal and quickly dispersed to the fields, the pastureland, the barn and the construction site. In the town and on the valley floor they worked with a will beneath the bright, pleasantly warm sun.

Edge, the stranger in their midst, was the lone idler. Sitting and smoking and reflecting that since his tragically short marriage to Elizabeth, he had been as celibate as the hard-working men of Paradise. But, he concluded his thoughts sardonically, this strange town filled with religious maniacs was not the place to seek fulfilment of the renewed natural urges supplanted by the passage of time upon lessening grief.

"What do I owe you, feller?" he asked, rising as the man with the pock-marked face led the stallion out from the forge section of the stable.

"Whatever you can afford to pay will be placed in the cathedral fund," Angel Francis replied.

"What you do with it is your business," Edge said, reaching into his hip pocket and pulling out his bankroll. The stack of bills was a large one, the money earned dangerously. But the work had not been hard, for killing came easy to the half-breed. He was aware of the avaricious look cast at the better than a thousand dollers by Angel Francis. He counted off three singles.

"Figure four bits a shoe and a single for your trouble," Edge said, handing the money into the man's sweaty, sooted palm.

"The horse has been fed and watered."

Edge shrugged and gave him another dollar. "For the feed. Water falls free from the sky. Horse did the work eating."

"I will not quarrel with that."

"Need supplies, feller."

"Over at the barn. I will show you, sinner."

He started across the street, boots raising puffs of dust, for the thirsty earth had quickly sucked up the morning's rain. Edge pocketed the wad of bills and took the Winchester from against the stable wall before following him.

The barn was only that at one end, where the double doors of a loading bay gave entrance to an area half-filled with cut stone blocks, the other half crammed with animal feed, crates of canned food, bins of flour and bolts of black serge. An aisle ran down the centre and at the far end opened out into a temporary church with neatly aligned pews and an altar and pulpit at the front.

"We need a place in which to worship the Lord until the cathedral is erected," Angel Francis explained when he saw the half-breed looking towards the church section. "Arch Angel Luke has consecrated the building."

"He's a guy with a lot of pull," the half-breed muttered and swung towards where Sarah and Edith waited behind a short length of store counter.

One of the women returned his cool gaze with tight-lipped displeasure. The other one, with the thinner face, paler skin and deep green eyes, surveyed him with a strange kind of detached interest. Once he had been an undeniably handsome boy. But the horrors of war and the ravages of violence which had tracked him across the peacetime years into adulthood had left their marks on his face. Not altering the basic structure of the dual-heritage features, but changing their set in some subtle fashion to underlay them with a brooding cruelty. Many women found the latent evil repulsive; others discovered themselves inexorably attracted to the man, often without realising the nature of the sexual magnet.

Now he sensed the vibrations emanating from the searching eyes of the woman and he showed her a cynical smile. "It ain't ever worth dying for, angel," he said. "All I want from you is some jerked beef, beans and coffee."

The woman flushed and the colour was further proof of how attractive she could be had she not chosen this way of life.

"He has money to pay, Angel Sarah," the black-clad man at the half-breed's side said. "I will leave you now."

The man went out of the barn with undue haste which detracted from the dignity of his clothing.

"Payment is not demanded from sinners," the stern-faced woman said frostily. "If tendered freely it helps to atone for their sins."

"Pay the going rate for the supplies," Edge told her with an easy grin. "Don't reckon the Treasury's got enough of what it takes to buy me into heaven."

"The more you mock, the harder becomes the path to atonement," the woman admonished as Angel Sarah began to gather together the half-breed's order.

"Guess you don't stock tobacco?"

"A tool of the Devil."

Angel Sarah was stronger than she looked. She hefted cartons and crates on to the counter with smooth ease. Edge told her the number of each item he required and she had to take great effort to avoid meeting his appraising gaze as she took out the cans and sacks. The half-breed dug into his hip pocket again and drew out the bankroll.

"Figure ten dollars covers it," he said.

"And the rest to pay your fine, sinner," Arch Angel Luke boomed.

Edge whirled from the counter, sliding from a casual posture to a rigid, half crouched attitude. The Winchester was aimed from the hip, the metallic scraping of the lever action adding sound to his movement. Luke stood in the centre of the open doorway, flanked by Angel Francis on one side and Prophet Thomas on the other. Half a dozen other men were grouped behind the blank-faced trio. None of them was armed.

"Guess nothing is just as good as empty guns," Edge said softly. The palm of his hand held the money hard against the rifle stock as his finger took first pressure on the trigger. The barrel swung from left to right and came to rest drawing a bead on Luke. "Be a pity if you get killed for nothing."

"We had a meeting in the fields," Luke said, ignoring the Winchester and the half-breed's threatening words. "It was agreed not to harm you, sinner. Thus we fulfill our promise to allow you freedom. But you interfered with the Lord's work and must pay for that. Pay in money in the form of a fine."

Edge curled back his lips in a cold grin. "Mighty fast meeting after you heard about my bankroll."

"It is the Lord's will we should know of it," Luke argued flatly. "I ask that you pay the fine peaceably in the knowledge the money will be put to good use."

"No deal, feller. I got my own good uses for it."

"So be it."

It was Angel Angus who had entered the long building through the church entrance and climbed silently to the top of the stock of cut-stone blocks. Then inched along in the confined space beneath the roof, to squat in readiness immediately above where Edge stood. Angel Luke lifted a bony hand to his face and rubbed the side of his nose with a skinny finger. The Scotsman saw the signal and acted.

Crouched on the very edge of the uppermost layer of blocks, he simply tipped himself forward. As he fell, he stretched out his arms to their full length, curling his hands into talons. The men in the sunlit doorway stared intently at the half-breed, not betraying by the flicker of an eyelid what was happening. Thus, it was that sixth sense for danger—a necessity for the professional survivor—which warned Edge. And an instant later a stirring of displaced air told him the direction from which the threat came.

Ice-cold anger showed in his abruptly narrowed eyes as he took a long stride forward, pivoted on his leading foot and angled the rifle upwards. He saw the diving man but did not recognise him. What he saw was a man seeking to disarm and perhaps destroy him. To Edge there was just one instinctive response. The moment the Winchester swung on to the target, the finger tightened on the trigger. The crack of the exploding bullet was very loud in the well-stocked barn. The shell drilled through the top of Angus's head, seared a killing course through his brain, smashed through the roof of his mouth and exited beneath his chin. He became limp with death while still in mid-air and crumpled like a rag doll at the feet of his killer. His head was twisted to exhibit his face. There was a bubbling of welling blood in his gaping mouth. Then the crimson liquid exploded upwards as the impact of the fall squeezed the breath from his lungs into his throat.

"I warned you!" Prophet Thomas squeaked as Edge whirled again, raking rifle and eyes across the forms of the petrified women and then faced the shocked group in the doorway. "I prophecied this sinnner would bring tragedy to Paradise. Did I not say he was experienced in spreading all manner of violent death?"

"Always ready to widen my range, little man," the half-breed rasped. "First time I ever shot an angel on the wing."

CHAPTER FOUR

"How the friggin' hell do they keep this barge afloat?" Forrest growled softly as the seven Union men and the two Rebels rested, waist-deep in water, under the bank at the corner of the wharf.

"Don't reckon it does," Bell muttered. "Restin' on the mud. Just there to kid the city folk the South's got a navy."

The ironclad had certainly seen better days. She was a converted sternwheeler, her former superstructure stripped and replaced with a citadel of iron sheeting. The citadel was slitted at four points along each side and two in the forward section. The ugly snouts of 15-inch smoothbore cannon angled out through the ports. The armoured pilothouse was at the stern, forward of the tall smokestack. Aligned in front of this was a line of four tub-shaped mortars calibrated for 13-inch shells—two angled to port and two to starboard. The entire ship—iron superstructure and wooden hull—was painted grey, but it was peeling in many places and patches of red rust showed elsewhere. A hole in the port bow just above the waterline had been roughly patched. Other signs of an old battle were deep dents and a few cracks in the citadel. The refit seemed to make her top heavy on the rising tide and her broad beam suggested she would be unable to make more than a few knots without danger of floundering.

Surveying the ship, which had the inappropriate name of *Southern Glory* lettered in faded white on the forward plating of the pilothouse, Captain Hedges had personal doubts about the viability of a riverborne escape from Richmond. But it did have in its favour the element of the unexpected. Soon, the governor's disappearance would be noticed and the time-lag until his body was found was unlikely to be long. Within moments the alarm would be given about the escaped prisoners and—in view of the importance attached to the capture of the Union troopers—no effort would be spared to find them. It was conceivable that all land exits from the city would be sealed before anybody thought about the James River as an escape route.

"Any of you men ever worked on a riverboat?" Hedges asked.

"My brother Henry gambled on the Mississippi steamers before the war," Rhett muttered sourly, his groin beginning to ache again, worse than before now that the numbing effect of the chill water had gone.

"Don't reckon the Rebs'll ante up their tub in a poker game," Hedges rasped. "Any man wants to do it the hard way, the sea's in that direction."

He crouched down and launched himself away from the bank, striking out with powerful crawl strokes.

"This is gonna be easy?" Forrest growled rhetorically, then pushed away from the bank in the wake of the Captain.

Floyd and Myron went next, prodded out into deep water by Bell and Scott.

"I don't swim so good," Rhett moaned.

"So drown," Seward said with a scowl as he pushed away from the bank.

"But don't start yellin' 'til you're goin' down for the third time, Bob," Douglas told the nervous New Englander.

Rhett found his courage from the sight of the other men swimming silently away from him, leaving him alone at the bank. Then, with a boost provided by a backward glance towards the top of the gallows visible above the prison fence, he plunged out into deep water. He dog-paddled, not daring to open his mouth to take in air.

Hedges led the men around the bow of the ironclad and along the centre-river, port side, to the framework supporting the big sternwheel. A glance along the wharf showed it to be deserted. It was too early for the civilian working day to have started and a naval guard was apparently regarded as unnecessary in the Confederate capital.

All traces of night had varnished now and the white mist wisping up from the river to form a low cloud ceiling did not look strong enough to present much of a barrier against the soon-to-rise sun. On the far side of the river, the background hum of the city was already beginning to increase in volume as the citizens of Richmond awoke at the start of a new day

"We need guns and ammo," Hedges said to the men clinging to the support around him. "We don't need noisy trouble."

"Maybe that part ain't up to us," Douglas pointed out, then added a belated: "Sir."

Hedges ignored him to direct a hard, narrow-eyed stare at Myron and Floyd—the latter less foul-smelling after the swim. "You fellers understand what I say?" he rasped.

Myron nodded.

Floyd scowled. "I ain't gonna kill none of my own people, Yankee."

"Touching," Hedges said softly, and reached up towards the higher support for the sternwheel. But he didn't make contact. Instead, his arm crooked, hand darting under the dripping hair at the back of his head. The razor came free of the pouch. Bell kicked away from the stern of the ship and lunged to the side, going behind the terrified Myron. Treading water, he hauled the Rebel under the surface. Floyd tried to throw himself backwards, but he banged against the solid obstruction of the grinning Scott. Still holding on to the support with one hand, Hedges stabbed the razor sideways. Beating at the water to stay afloat, Floyd had no defence. The blade, powered by Hedges' fist, skimmed across the water and sank to the hilt in Floyd's throat. The windpipe was holed, cutting off the scream before it could start. Then the honed steel sliced through the jugular vein. Blood billowed like red smoke in the water.

It was over in the space of three seconds, with the razor nestling back in the neck pouch.

"Him down, him up!" Hedges rasped, pointing first at Scott, then at Bell.

Scott drew in a deep breath and plunged for the river bed, helped by the dead weight of Floyd. Bell moved back to the stern for a handhold and dragged the gasping Myron up to where he could breathe again. The rising tide swept Floyd's diluted blood upstream.

"Your brother was an idealist, feller," Hedges told Myron. "He wasn't in the war long enough to live without all that honour crap."

"He's dead?" Myron croaked, snapping his head to left and right, searching for his brother.

"It's the only thing to be when you can't live," Hedges told him. "Your decision. This tub ain't no passenger ship, feller."

"I got outta the war so I wouldn't have to kill," Myron groaned.

"Him, too, Captain?" Bell asked with an excited grin.

"Just watch him close, trooper," Hedges replied. "It ain't what you say, its, the way that you say it."

Then, with another fast glance along the dock, Hedges climbed up on to the sternwheel supports and on to the narrow strip of decking surrounding the citadel. The others followed him, Scott breaking surface to be the last man aboard.

"You fixed him so he won't float up?" Forrest rasped.

Scott grinned evilly as he squeezed water from his sodden clothes. "He won't be comin' up for awhile, Frank."

The entrance hatch to the citadel was aft, between the rear of the pilothouse and the smokestack. It was latched, but not locked. Hedges eased it open a crack and peered inside while the others cast steady or nervous glances along the dock.

"You know somethin', Captain?" Seward said.

But Hedges whirled on him and drove him into silence with a piercing look from his ice-blue eyes. Then he eased the hatchway open further and invited the men to look through. He had been wrong in thinking the ironclad had been left unguarded. The citadel was long and narrow, with barred grilles in the low overhead bulkhead to admit light and air. Running down the centre was a continuous line of store bins filled with shells and primers for the cannon and mortars. Four Rebel seaman were seated on the decking, their backs resting against the bins. All of them were soundly asleep. An empty bottle was held upright between the thighs of one of the men.

"What's the penalty for sleeping on the job in a war situation, Captain?" Forrest whispered.

"First one for you, sergeant," Hedges hissed. "Bell, take the second. Seward, the third. The others come inside and cream Myron if he even breathes too loud."

He went through the hatchway first and the others slid in after him, Forrest, Bell and Seward moving into a single file to line themselves up for the kill. Rhett closed the hatchway silently while Douglas and Scott made a human sandwich of the terrified Myron.

Hedges led the way along the deck on the opposite side from the sleeping seamen, moving soundlessly on the balls of his feet. Their victims slept in a short line, only a few inches between them. Their holstered revolvers had been visible from the hatchway, but it was not until the Union men were immedately behind the sailors, leaning over the bins, that they saw the rifles lying on the decking.

Sweat beads erupted from tension-opened pores to mix with the droplets of river water held amongst the stubble on the troopers' faces. Hedges sensed the three pairs of impatient eyes directed at him. He knew each man was itching for the kill and burning with desire to feel the cold metal of a gun in his hands again. It was just a few short hours since they had last possessed fire-power and experienced the evil excitation of seeing men die at their hands. But to the troopers, who could not recall any other kind of existence, bringing death to others was all they lived for. Each minute of enforced idleness with empty hands had been stretched into an hour. Hedges knew how they felt, for he was as one with them.

His movements were slow as he withdrew the razor and arched his tall frame further across the bins. The trio of troopers moved in mirror-like imitations of him. Then, with rasped sighs of relish, they matched the Captain's speed. Their hands clawed, they folded forward, bellies and chests resting on the bins. Then the hands swung together and fastened around the exposed necks of the sleeping seaman. Each victim awoke with a gasp of alarm that became a muted, choked scream of terror and pain. Arms were flung up and bodies writhed. But sleep had taken too great a part of a second to shake off. The strangling hands of the troopers were too firmly fixed to surrender to the scratching, tearing attacks of the seamen's fingers. As the men's complexions turned to red and then purple and their tongues protruded from gaping mouths, their eyes swivelled up to look into the coldly grinning faces of their killers.

"Wanna get rid of a battleship?" Bell rasped.

"Hello, sailor," Seward whispered and giggled.

"Army beats the Navy four to nothin'," Forrest growled a moment before the men died, legs and torsos becoming still, hands falling away and eyes clouding opaque then closing.

Each trooper held his victim a few seconds more, making certain of death. Then they let go. A trio of death rattles sounded in the throats as deflating lungs expelled final breaths. Then, snatching the Confederate Colts from the holsters of the dead men and scooping up the Spencer rifles from the deck, the three troopers straightened.

"Only three to nothing, maybe," Hedges said softly.

He was in the same, over-the-bins attitude as the others had been, but was using the razor rather than his bare hands, and the fourth seaman was still alive. He was bleeding a little, but not fatally. Hedges' left hand was on the top of the man's head, bunching tufts of sandy hair in a fist. The right was clasped around the handle of the razor, which was shoved two inches up the man's nostril, honed edge angled inwards. The thin rivulet of crimson had its source in a minor nick in the tender membranes under the bridge. The man's hands were splayed, palms down, on the deck. He didn't move, not even breathing. His lips were pressed tight together, seemingly sealed by the sticky blood oozing over them. His eyes bulged so much they seemed on the point of popping from his head. His youth made his terror more pathetic. He could not be more than seventeen.

"He's a cute kid, Captain," Forrest allowed in a sour tone as he ran his hand lovingly over the Spencer. "But you've killed his kind before."

Hedges ignored the sergeant and bent his head to whisper softly in the ear of the terrified boy. "When's this tub scheduled to sail?"

"It . . . it ain't," the youngster stuttered. "Not for . . . for . . . days. Gotta have repairs."

"What needs fixing?" Hedges demanded softly. "Engine?"

"No. Citadel plating. Don't kill me, mister . . . please don't kill me. "

"Know how to run the engines, feller?"

"No, mister. I'm a gunner."

"That's a shame," Hedges mocked. "You got the wrong advice from the careers officer." He released the boy's head and jerked the razor out of his nostril. "Gunners we've got. Short on engineers."

The boy mistook the mocking tone for genuine compassion. Instead of reaching for his gun, he craned up his head to look at an upsidedown view of Hedges' impassive face. He read the look of the killer too late and the razor plunged into his exposed throat just as he began to scream. Hedges snatched the Confederate copy Colt from the holster a moment before the blood-gouting body toppled.

"Thought for a minute there you'd gone soft, Captain," Forrest said with a grin, swinging over the bins and dragging the boy's body off the rifle.

"Be obliged if you didn't make any more mistakes, sergeant," the Captain told him as Scott, Douglas and Rhett clustered around, eager to get a gun. "May not be time to make allowances for them from here on in."

"Hey, what's all the noise aboard?"

The troopers froze, eyes raking from the gunports overlooking the dock to the lone figure of Myron who had been left in front of the closed hatchway. As the gun muzzles swung in the same track as the eyes, Myron raised both hands to clamp over his mouth.

"Staying dumb is smart, Reb," Forrest hissed.

"You hear me?" the gruff voice called from outside.

"What I tried to tell you awhile back, Captain," Seward whispered. "There was this old guy comin' along the dock."

Holding the revolver low at his side, Hedges took long strides to the nearest gunport and peered down over the glinting cannon barrel—glinting because the rising sun had sent a first shaft of yellow light over the horizon to penetrate the mist.

The man standing on the dock, hands on hips and head cocked suspiciously to one side, was about sixty. He would have been skinny had it not been for his expansive waistline. His legs were short and bowed. His belly bulged and seemed to be sagging all the way down from beneath his scrawny neck. He had a small head, hung with a lot of loose skin, bald on top and grey-bearded at the jaw. The whites of his eyes were blood-shot around the bright grey pupils. He was dressed in oil-stained coveralls that had once been white.

"The guys were horsing around!" Hedges called, showing his face at the port, but not his sodden clothing.

"The one yelled like he wasn't havin' fun," the old-timer answered, and started up the unrailed gangplank connecting the dock with the ironclad.

"Little upset is all," Hedges told the man. "Guess something got up his nose."

When he turned around he saw that Myron still stood with both hands to his mouth, encouraged now by the revolver Rhett pressed into his belly. The other troopers were all armed, Forrest having retained the extra weapon to hold a Colt and a Spencer. Despite their dishevelled, water-dripping appearance, they looked alert, ready and willing for a fight.

"Prepare to repel boarder, sir?" Roger Bell said softly.

"This guy could earn his keep," Hedges answered, and strode towards the hatchway.

The old-timer's footfalls rang on the deck then halted. Hedges used a foot to thrust open the hatch. Then he sidestepped into the opening and pointed the revolver.

"Hell's bells, what's this?" the man said, his tone even, and showing his surprise by the merest lifting of his near hairless eyebrows.

"Don't ask for whom they toll, feller," Hedges said, and stepped back, motioning the newcomer to enter the citadel.

The man was older than he had looked, and Hedges re-estimated his age at seventy. For that number of years and the amount of excess weight he toted at his middle, he was remarkably well-preserved. And he moved smoothly. Unhurried, but without effort. He halted inside and eyed the troopers and Myron quizzically as Hedges closed the hatchway behind him.

Then he sniffed. "Gotta admire the gall of you guys, but you're gonna have trouble off-loading her once you've stole her."

"A friggin' commedian," Forrest rasped. He levelled the Spencer. "You tired of livin', old man?"

Another sniff, with a shrug this time. "Done most of what I wanted in my life, son," he answered, and nodded towards the sprawled bodies of the seamen. "Reckon it was tougher for them to die."

"What you doin' here this time in the morning?" Hedges demanded.

"Me and the rest of the repair crew don't get on, mister. All they can talk about is women and war. And I'm too old for both. So I like to get my chores done before they start."

"What chores?"

"Fixin' the engines of murdered old boats like the *Southern Glory*," the man answered, and for the first time there was a trace of emotion in his voice—sadness.

"Was told this tub didn't have engine trouble," Hedges said.

"All these navy boats got engine trouble after the way they're misused," the old timer replied. "Weren't built for the kind of treatment they get."

"Can you run an engine as well as fix it?"

The sniff was resonant with scorn. "I was captain, mate, engineer and roustabout on the Mississippi for more years than you been outta diapers, son," he muttered. "Ain't no chore on a sternwheeler I can't do."

"He ain't ready to die yet, Captain," Forrest growled, and showed his stained teeth in a grin.

"Captain of what?" the old-timer wanted to know.

"Union cavalry," Hedges told him. "Fresh out of a Rebel gaol and anxious to stay out."

"Abe Lincoln's got his points and I just happened to be visitin' kinfolk in Florida when the shootin' started. War don't mean nothin' to me except it pays me a few bucks. Sure would like to run an engine again, instead of just fixin' it."

"I ain't trusting you," Hedges warned.

"Wouldn't expect you to, son. Union don't make Captains from fools, I guess. I'll need a hand anyway. Just one. Other one can hold a gun on me."

"No fixing," Hedges said as the old-timer moved eagerly towards a companionway leading down into the bowels of the ironclad. "Just running. How long to get up a head of steam?"

"Take a navy guy an hour at least. Reckon I can do it in thirty minutes."

"Break a record without bursting a boiler," Hedges urged. "Go with him, Douglas. And treat him like your Pa unless he does something stupid."

Douglas spat. "I hated my Pa, sir. But I know what you mean."

The corporal trailed the old timer down the companionway and Hedges glanced around his men, selecting Seward and Scott, for their builds matched those of two of the dead seamen.

"Get into dry clothes," he ordered, and waved the Colt towards the inert bodies. "Theirs."

There were no gripes now. No references to Forrest for his opinion about Hedges' commands. The Captain had sprung them from Riverside Prison and secured a means of escape from Richmond. But, as Forrest had said earlier, they were still a long way from home. Until something went wrong that was in any way attributable to a mistake by the Captain, he was unquestionably in command. Like Seward and Scott, the other men listened in silence to the orders Hedges gave, and instantly complied. Even the tight-lipped Myron, who was assigned to the store bins.

Forrest and Bell were stationed at two cannons on the starboard side, overlooking the dock. Rhett went to a gun which commanded the open water of the river. Hedges took Seward and Scott outside the citadel and up into the pilothouse with him.

The controls were spartanly simple. A spoked wheel, a binnacle compass, an engine-room telegraph and a speaking tube. A brass telescope was clipped to a bulkhead. Hedges lifted the mouthpiece of the speaking tube and whistled into it.

"Chief-engineer Robert Chivers here, Captain," the old timer answered perkily. "I reckon this old engine'll get you to the ocean if you don't push her too hard."

"Just get up that steam and let me know if you think she's going to blow," Hedges told him, then swung around to face the two Union troopers in Confederate navy uniform. "You're in that gear because you'll be out in the open and there may be people around by the time we're ready to move. When I tell you, cast off the fore and aft lines, then man two of those mortars. There's got to be some way the shells can be passed up from below."

"Sure thing, sir," Seward acknowledged, checking the Colt was secure in his pants' belt.

Scott eyed the mortars with keen anticipation, then swung his gaze ruefully out across the river and over the sunlit roofs of Richmond. "Guess we don't have the range to lob a few shells into the Capitol, Captain?" he asked.

Hedges grinned. "Nobody'll blame you for trying, trooper," he said. "Except maybe the people you hit when the shells fall short."

"All of 'em Johnnie Rebs," Seward rasped.

There was nothing else to do or say then. Everything now depended upon the ancient Robert Chivers: and Hedges was inclined to believe the old-timer's neutrality could be swayed by an opportunity to relive his past as a riverboat crewman. Strangely, while the sun seemed to leap with unnatural haste above the eastern horizon, each passing minute appeared to drag many times its normal length. The mist evaporated and the sky was a clear blue, marred only by the ugly smudges of smoke curling up from the city's chimneys as the breakfast fires were lit. In the full, bright light of day, the faces of Seward and Scott were incongruous above the uniforms. Through the stubble of a day and a night, the grime of the tunnelling could be seen ingrained in the pores and the lines of skin old before its time. They looked weary, but oddly not weary—this due to the glitter in their eyes. The light of wildness that was close to lunacy.

But it was a reflection of the men's inner feelings which caused Hedges no anxiety. For he was familiar with it: had seen that look in the faces of all his men as the time for a fight grew imminent. He knew the feeling from his own experience and had no doubt his lean features also betrayed the pent-up excitement building inside him; being stoked, like the fire in the boiler below deck, for the moment of release. The fire would produce steam to power the big sternwheel of the ironclad. The excitement would be transformed into exhileration to drive the iron men into battle. But they were not iron men, of course. They were human flesh and blood with brains, minds, feelings and emotions. Killers they had become, able to blast their enemies into eternity without a moment's hesitation or a split-second of regret. Human beings committing inhuman atrocities which would surely send a normal man into the dark depths of insanity—unless he was protected.

And this is how Hedges regarded the pre-battle anticipation and the hell-for-leather intoxication during the unleashed savagery of war. As a defence mechanism of temporary insanity which guarded himself and his men against madness for all time.

A shout exploded from the compound behind the prison. Another answered the first and this was followed by a confused furore of sound as words poured from many lips.

"I think they've found their boss, sir," Seward said with a broad grin.

From the elevated position in the pilothouse Hedges could see over the perimeter fence into the compound, but the intervening bulk of the warehouse obstructed his view of the rear cell block and the area immediately behind it.

"We're still ahead in the game," the Captain answered.

"Here come some new players for their team," Scott rasped tensely.

He was looking out over the sternwheel and Hedges turned to follow the direction of his steady stare. Out along the dock to where a group of civilians in soiled dungarees were ambling through a gateway and turning towards the *Southern Glory*. Smart in contrast were four uniformed seamen with sidearms and ported rifles. The repair crew and the change of guard. Still two hundred yards away and apparently in no hurry to start work.

Hedges elevated his gaze and saw black woodsmoke curling from the smokestack, flecked with short-lived sparks. Good as an indication of the progress made by Chivers, but bad because the men on the dock were sure to spot it and recognise it as a sign something was wrong.

"Cast off!" Hedges snapped at the troopers. "Seward forward, Scott stern. Then get on those mortars and load up."

The order to action stations overcame Scott's nerves and both men went out of the pilothouse fast, sliding down the iron ladder and splitting to head for their assigned positions. Hedges whistled down the speaking tube.

"Chief-Engineer Rob——" Chivers begin.

"I know who you are!" Hedges snapped. "The guys you don't like and the change of guard are on their way down the dock, feller. I'm cutting this tub loose from the dock. Sooner you can get the wheel turning, less chance we'll have of being crunched against the pilings by the tide."

His voice was calm but authoritative. But, as Chivers had already proved, he was not the kind of man who needed soothing in a crisis.

"Tide's about ready to turn, son," the old-timer replied cheerfully. "She'll drift downstream. Keep the wheel hard to port. You'll have power soon as I can give it to you."

Grinning at the old man's unruffled attitude, Hedges spun the wheel to its fullest extent and then shoved the telegraph to its FULL AHEAD setting. The signal bells made a pleasant tinkling sound.

"Didn't reckon you'd want anything else," he heard Chivers acknowledge, his voice far off from the end of the free-hanging speaking tube.

As he saw Seward free the bow line, Hedges realised the noise of shouting from the prison had ceased. Then, as he swung around to see what progress Scott was making, whistles began to shrill and a warning bell clanged. Scott had been unable to loosen the stern line from the deck cleat. He was monkeying down the line, ankles locked over it and propelling himself with his hands.

"What the friggin' hell?"

The shout came from the group on the dock, which had halted. They could see the bow of the boat swinging towards mid-river, stretching the stern line taut to give Scott a stable way down. Hedges cursed—at the fact of the razor being snug in the pouch instead of Scott's hands, and at the arrival of the Rebels which negated the advantage of surprise in the river escape.

The gap between hull and dock widened and the gangplank splashed into the oil-smoothed water in between. Scott reached the dock, hauled himself up and crouched at the bollard to tug on the rope.

"Hand me up some shells, you Reb bastard?!"

This from Seward, who was squatting beside the central mortar. He had folded back a hinged plate and was reaching down into the citadel. Hedges saw him bring up two big shells, load one and rest the other. Then Seward reached down for more.

"Hey! You!"

The men on the dock were running now but Scott's stolen uniform caused the naval guard to hold their fire. Chivers, or perhaps Douglas, shouted something into the speaking tube, but the creaking of the boat, the slap of water on her hull and the clatter of running feet deluged the words with noise. The line splashed into the river. Scott made a louder smack diving in after it. The big sternwheel began to turn.

The motion of the boat, Hedges thought, but then he felt the decking tremble. He heard the throb of the engine. The wheel began to thrash at the water. A volley of shots exploded and bullets clanged against the armour plating of the pilothouse. The *Southern Glory* angled hard away from the dock. Hedges spun the wheel for a mid-river course and glanced back over his shoulder.

The men on the dock had halted: the repair crew staring in awe after the departing boat, the seamen crouched on one knee. firing from the shoulder. Hedges caught a brief glimpse of Scott skimming through the white water of the chruning wake, hanging on with both hands to the trailing stern line. Then something bulky obstructed his view for a moment. There was a thump, diminished by the engine and water sounds, then an awful crunching noise. More rifle shots cracked. Three bullets clanged against the pilothouse. A lucky shot whined through a rear port and ricochetted off the binnacle. Hedges cursed as he felt the thud of impact and warmth of blood behind his left shoulder.

He checked he was holding course, then glanced behind him again. Scott was closing with the boat, hauling himself hand-over-hand, approaching the danger area of the threshing wheel. The white water bubbling around him was streaked with dark crimson diluting to pink. But the blood was not spilling from Scott. It came from countless wounds in the mutilated body of Floyd—the object which had interrupted Hedges' view a few moments earlier.

Scott had fixed the dead Rebel to a strut on the sternwheel, unbuckling the man's belt then refastening it around the wood. Thus, with each turn of the wheel, the body was hauled out of the water flung through the top arc and then plunged down again. But the gap between wheel and stern was not wide enough and engine power always overcame frail human flesh and bone. Floyd's head and one arm had been torn off. Both legs were broken at the knees and jagged ends of bone pierced flesh. Each time the body smashed down on to the stern more chunks of human meat were ripped from the torso. And, each time the wheel threw its burden across the top arc, a spray of watered-down blood lashed the pilothouse, like rain gusted by wind.

"Scott, you stupid bastard!" Hedges yelled through a side

port after another volley of rifle fire spat at the pilothouse. "The Reb could have fouled something and wrecked the wheel!"

"I got my own friggin' problems, sir!" Scott snarled back breathlessly. "Get someone to give me a hand for Christ's sake!"

"Everyone's busy!" Hedges yelled as the remains of Floyd were dragged clear of the water again. But this time the belt holding him a prisoner snapped and momentum tossed the broken body high into the air. Without the burden, the wheel plunged into a faster rate and the boat surged forward.

The body splashed into the river at the precise moment Seward fired the mortar. The shell left the muzzle with a deafening crack. It lobbed through the morning air with a shrill whistle. The fusillade of rifle shots seemed more distant than the group of men on the dock. The shell scored a direct hit on one of the seamen. It smashed an enormous hole through his chest and exploded inside him as he was flung to the ground. A pall of black smoke obliterated the group for a moment. Then the blast cleared it. Whole bodies and torn sections sailed away from the impact point. Arms, legs, hands, feet and at least two heads seemed suspended in the sunlight for long moments, dropping sprays and gouts of bright crimson. Then they splashed cleanly into the river or spattered with renewed bursts of blood against the concrete dock or timber walls of the warehouse.

Three of the seamen and two civilians had been torn apart by the explosion. The fourth sailor and three civilians remained whole, but lay in the oddly twisted, utterly inert attitudes of certain death. The remainder writhed in agony or were held unmoving prisoners to shock, groaning and screaming for help.

Seward was doing a gleeful dance of triumph beside the killing mortar. "Frank!'" he shrieked in delight. "Frank, I got the bastards. Right in the goddamn middle of 'em. Spread 'em all over the goddamn dock."

Scott hauled himself along the final few feet of rope and clambered up on to the deck. He flopped out full-length, gasping for air to revitalise exhausted lungs.

"You see it, Captain?" Seward yelled, staring with excited eyes at the pilothouse. "I sure as hell creamed them Johnnie Rebs, uh?"

"Sure, Billy," Hedges called in reply as he became aware of a burning pain behind his left shoulder. "With someone with your luck on our side, the Union's just got to win this war."

"One shell was all it took! Crrruuunch!"

"One shell," Hedges agreed in a murmur only he could hear, his exhilaration overriding the pain of the shoulder wound. "And the Rebs just went to pieces."

"It is the punishment of the Lord," the white-haired Arch-Angel Luke said simply. "And verification that He does not approve violence in the doing of His work. The Angels of Paradise regret it was our actions which caused you to kill our brother, sinner."

The cemetery was peacefully sited among trees to one side of the town. Edge had attended the burial service for Angel Angus because it was pleasant to sit astride the stallion in the cool shade before moving out into the hot sun of afternoon. The whole population of Paradise were present, standing bowed-head and silent amid many simple wooden crosses marking the graves of Angels who had died less violently than this newest entrant from earthly to heavenly paradise.

The citizens' firm belief that every event was pre-ordained had rapidly countered the shock at the shooting in the barn and the half-breed had not been molested again. While the body was removed and the grave dug. Sarah and Edith had completed Edge's order. Then he had used the forge fire in the blacksmith section of the stables to heat some beans and boil water for coffee. When he emerged to saddle the stallion, the town and the fields spread out below it were deserted. Luke's booming voice, intoning a prayer over the body of Angus had drawn him to the cool grove of trees by the cemetery. Now, the short, simple burial service was over and Luke, backed by the regular group which seemed to be members of some kind of council, appeared to be attempting an apology to Edge. But the expression of regret and laying the incident at the doorstep of the Lord's will was as far as he got.

Then, as the half-breed gave a curt nod of acknowledgement, Luke held up a staying hand.

"You owe us no favours, sinner," he intoned. "But we would deem it one if you did not talk of Paradise on your travels. Few sinners discover this valley. When one does, it invariably results in trouble."

Edge shook his head. "I only talk when there's good reason to say something, feller," he replied. "Ain't no good reason to talk about this place."..

Luke lowered his hand. The men backing him dispersed first, and then the lesser angels of Paradise moved out of the grove after them.

"We especially would not wish the law to know of Paradise, sinner," the white-haired old man said. "We live by the Lord's rules which do not always match those made by man. Just one of the reasons why the Earthly Angels have chosen to isolate themselves from the rest of humanity."

"I especially don't talk with lawman," Edge told him with a wry smile, thinking fleetingly of a time, long ago, when he had worn a badge.* "Same reason."

He tugged gently on the reins to turn the stallion away from Luke, then tapped the animal lightly with his heels to walk him across the grove. Behind him, as a sign of democracy at work in Paradise, Arch Angel Luke picked up a spade and began to shovel the displaced soil back into the grave. There was no thud of earth on wood for the townspeople did not waste cut timber on caskets; nor did they discard serviceable clothing. Angus went out of the world as naked as he came into it and the worms had direct access to his flesh. It was only his soul that concerned the angels.

Edge stayed in the shade of the trees for a long time, but the incline of the valley's western side was steep and he and his horse were in a heavy sweat when they emerged at the top. The terrain forced him to swing south for a while, parallel with the valley.

**See—Edge: Ten Thousand Dollars American.*

But, because of the height of the intervening trees, it was not until he reached a man-made break that he was able to look down upon Paradise and the neat fields spread out before it. His vantage point was the overhang—execution rock—three hundred feet above the medieval punishment area.

He pursed his lips as he leaned forward, around the neck of the horse, to peer directly down. The animal was nervous at being so close to the lip of the precipice, his nostrils flared and ears pricked. The half-breed's long-fingered, brown hand stroked the lathered horseflesh gently and his tone was soothing. "There but for the will of the Lord . . . "

A rifle shot, diminished by distance, caused him to curtail the wry comment. It was followed immediately by a shrill scream which sounded even further away. But he saw the woman fall, toppling from the highest section of the cathedral wall where she had been mortaring a new block of stone into place. Despite the distance, Edge could tell it was a woman who had been shot. For, as she crumpled, her long black skirt was hoisted to her waist displaying the whiteness of her legs. Angus had been that stark pallor all over.

For stretched seconds, the entire population of Paradise seemed frozen into a state of suspended animation. In the fields and pasture and on the construction site, men and women raised themselves from their chores and stared across the river. In the town they stepped from the doorways of the buildings and shaded their eyes from the sunlight to peer in the same direction.

Then, with obscene terror, the brief interlude of shocked silence was shattered. They came out of the trees on the far side of the river and plunged into the slow-moving, sun-dappled water: shrieking, laughing and firing wildly with rifles and revolvers. There were twenty of them. Spokan indians, dressed in rags and with their naked torsos and faces garishly daubed with warpaint. Riding ill-cared-for, sweating ponies that took to the cool water with eagerness and then snorted and tossed their heads in protest at the demand for speed.

The half-breed's narrowed eyes changed the direction and focus of their cool gaze and showed no trace of emotion at what they saw. The people of Paradise were no longer held immobile by shock. They were running in full-scale retreat from the attacking indians. Age dictated the pace and those with the greater stamina of fewer years held back to help the older ones. The river was deep and the ponies were weary. The inital burst of continuous gunfire slackened as the riders were forced to concentrate on driving their ponies through the water. But four more black-garbed forms were already sprawled in the field of growing wheat, blasted to death as they whirled to run. And two more—an old man stumbling along with an arm around an older woman—pitched to the ground as sporadic shooting cracked from the group of indians.

The impassively watching half-breed became aware that, after the first few moments of terror, the element of panic had left the fleeing townspeople. Although still powered by fear, there was purpose in the flight. The hooded-eyed gaze foreshortened again, to look down at the town. And it was apparent that the Earthly Angels were putting a contingency plan into operation. For every pair of running feet was directed towards the church entrance.

A loud splash drew Edge's attention back to the far side of the river and he uttered a non-committal grunt at what he saw. A heavily-laden flatbed wagon drawn by a six-horse team had plunged into the water at full-tilt. Estes Mackinlay had control of the reins while Silas Gabb lashed at the team with a horsewhip.

"Let's move it, feller," Edge said softly into the pricked ears of the stallion as he backed the animal away from the lip of the rock overhang. "All hell's breaking loose in Paradise."

CHAPTER FIVE

"THIS tub ain't got no sun deck, Scott!" Hedges yelled from the pilothouse. "Get off your back and man a gun, trooper."

Scott was still sprawled out flat on the trembling deck just forward of the churning sternwheel, panting to recover his breath after his struggle to climb aboard. He grimaced, preparing to snarl a grasping retort. But then a renewed burst of rifle fire chattered above the steady rumble of the ironclad's engine. Splinters exploded from the wood of the hull and deck and bullets ricochetted off the iron citadel. Fear for his life and the urge to retaliate exploded a shriek of anger from Scott's gaping mouth and sent a bolt of energy through his weary body. He sprang to his feet and dived into the cover of the pilothouse.

Hedges, his teeth bared and his eyes glittering as he battled mentally against the throbbing pain in his wounded shoulder, spun the wheel one-handed. The top-heavy *Southern Glory* responded sluggishly to the demand of her rudder, her bows nosing reluctantly towards the north bank of the river. She was churning past the compound behind the prison and it was from here that the new burst of gunfire was coming.

Guards, reinforced by a unit of soldiers assigned to assist with preparations for the public hanging, had taken only moments to link the prison break-out with the shooting at the docks. Now, using the seven graves as slit-trenches, they raked the slow-moving ironclad with a constant barrage of rifle fire.

"Jesus Christ, Captain, you spoiled my friggin' shot!"

The voice was that of Forrest, loud and vibrant with frustration. Gritting his teeth harder against the pain, Hedges rasped a curse, directed at himself, as he spun the wheel in the opposite direction. He blamed the burning agony of the wound for marring his judgement—causing him to react instinctively to the new attack without taking all circumstances into consideration.

The sudden change of course had slowed the ironclad, presenting the Rebels with an easier mark and swinging her cannon off target. And it gained nothing, for the James River was not wide enough to allow the sternwheeler out of rifle range as she churned past the prison. It was just the kind of error Forrest was likely to capitalise on. But at the moment the mean-faced sergeant was concerned with other things.

"That's friggin' better!" he yelled gleefully.

The comment was punctuated by the double crash of two cannon as he and Bell fired in unison. The deep roar muted the rifle fire and then stopped it as the Rebels ducked low into the graves. The shells whistled out of the grey puffs of muzzle smoke on a too-high trajectory, sailing across the water and the compound. Two rifles began to spit death from the boat and Hedges saw that Scott had scrambled up beside one of the mortars. He and Seward were sprawled out on their bellies, able to fire from the elevated position atop the citadel into the graves. Two Rebels twisted upright, clutching at faces from which blood was gouting. Then the cannon shells smashed into the wall of the cell block. Chunks of rock and shards of shrapnel rained down out of the upsurge of black smoke.

Two more shells roared from the cannon. The Rebels stayed crouched in the graves. Seward fired his mortar and Scott was only a moment later after stealing a shell from the younger man's stock. One of the cannon shells smashed into the gallows, reducing it to matchwood. The other pounded into the hole made by a previous shot and the rear wall of the cell block was breached. Both mortar shots dropped into a single grave.

"Billy, with your luck I ain't never gonna play poker with you," Hedges rasped as, for the second time in a few minutes, he saw whole and torn pieces of human bodies sail through the air.

It was as if the kill-crazy youngster had been able to hear the soft spoken words. He snatched his rifle and waved it triumphantly in the air as he grinned up at the pilothouse. "One's lucky maybe, Captain!" he yelled. "But two's just gotta be skill."

"You've got a natural knack for killing, trooper!" Hedges allowed as another cannon roared.

This time the puff of smoke spumed from the port side of the ironclad. The shell whistled across the river surface for a short distance, low down. Then it splashed into the water and thudded against the side of an anchored barge.

"Good old Bob!" Scott yelled. "He's got this natural bent for shootin' off behind other men."

"It's going down!" Rhett shrilled in delight.

Seward and Scott confined their responses to a fit of giggling, then flung themselves to the deck as the Rebels poured rifle fire towards the *Southern Glory* again.

"Get on the mortars!" Hedges roared as he realised the thrashing progress of the ironclad had carried her fixed cannon off target.

But, sickened into fury by the sight of the blood-soaked bodies of their shattered buddies, the men in the graves gave the exposed troopers no chance to load and prime the guns. Repeating rifles poured a deadly hail of lead across the length of the citadel. Pressing themselves hard against the rusted and dented iron, Scott and Seward bellied forward to duck into the cover of the narrow strip of decking on the port side.

"It was luck I'll allow, Captain!" Seward yelled. "And I ain't pushin' it no more."

The sight and sound of a constant stream of bullets crashing into the decking around the mortars and whining into ricochets held Hedges back from ordering the men to the guns a second time.

Rhett's cannon fired again and the shell burst into the wall of a riverside shack. A man screamed and lunged out through the doorway, staring down at the stump of bloody meat where his left arm had been attached to his body. Seward drew a bead on the fleeing man and put a bullet in his head. The man fell in the same direction as the spout of his own blood.

"Me and Bob make a great team!" Seward yelled at Scott. "He sets 'em running' and I pick 'em off."

A sudden eruption of shouting drew Hedges' attention to the activity on the south bank of the river again. The rifle fire fell off as the sounds from throats rose. He had to look over his shoulder and through an aft port as the ironclad churned down-river, sliding inexorably beyond the perimeter fence of the compound. But there was time to see what had happened. Emaciated prisoners, dressed in rags and begrimed with filth, had climbed through the breached wall of the cell block and dropped into the compound. Then, gaining strength from the heady experience of freedom after long incarceration, they had run for the graves and plunged down to the attack. Hands, clawed into talons or bunched into firsts, fought for possession of the rifles and revolvers. Then, as more prisoners poured from the shell-ravaged wall, the shooting began again. But this time the range was point-blank. And, where there was not even the room to bring a gun to bear, rifle stocks and revolver butts were raised and powered down. Lead ripped into hearts and tore through intestines. Skulls caved in under the assult of machined wood. Uniforms signified authority and it did not matter if a man was a prison guard or a soldier. He died. And sometimes this was not enough. More bullets and more vicious blows were pounded into unfeeling flesh.

Another shell whistled away from Rhett's gun and the New Englander uttered a shrill shriek of delight as he scored a direct hit on the head of a milk cow grazing peacefully at the lush grass of a waterside meadow. The animal's dead legs supported the headless body for a full second before collapsing.

"Tell dead-eyed dick cows are neutral in this war!" Hedges yelled as Scott and Seward got tentatively to their feet, peering around them for sign of a fresh attack.

Scott spat off the deck into the river. "Bob reckons all women are cows, sir," he drawled, his voice loud in the relative peace as the hand-to-hand fighting in the compound came to an end.

"Maybe sinking that barge sent him loony," Seward suggested

with a grin. "He ain't never hit nothin' with any kind of gun before."

"He sure enough scored a hit, though," Scott announced, peering back upriver to where the barge had half-filled with water through the shell hole. "Must have known it was a guy like Bob." The list of the barge increased abruptly and then, with a hiss of escaping air and a gurgle of inrushing water, she turned turtle. "Hey, will you look at that, Bob!" Scott yelled. "Bottoms up, boy!"

"We free and clear, Captain?" This from Forrest, hoisting himself up on to the citadel through the grating Seward had opened to get his supply of shells. His face was sooted with gun-smoke, which had the effect of brightening the evil glint in his grinning eyes as he sucked in the fresh, river air. Then he pulled himself completely from the hole and looked all round him.

The south bank of the river offered no threat. The few buildings beyond the prison had petered out and the vista was a broad one of the rolling fields of Virginia. Stretching so flat and featureless than a train could be seen hauling west along the tracks of the Richmond and Petersburg Railroad two miles away. To the north was a residential area of the city: expensive-looking frame and brick-built houses set back behind a strip of swampy meadowland. Donwstream, to where the river curled around a bluff, it was open country all the way.

"Unless the Rebs have got half a dozen frigates waiting for us the other side of that high ground, I reckon we're clear for awhile," Hedges called in reply.

"But you ain't authorising no deck tennis, right Captain?" Forrest said with a grin.

"Just appointing a ship's doctor," Hedges told him. "That's you, sergeant. Come up here and dig this lead out of my shoulder."

Forrest's grin broadened. To Hedges, who was suddenly feeling no pain as numbness set in, the sergeant's tobacco-stained teeth seemed to stretch from ear to ear. It was still early morning and only an Eastern spring. Yet the pale sun felt as if it was blazing down out of a desert sky at noon.

"That's the third friggin' time Hedges' has been hit," Seward said in a whisper.

But, in his oddly light-headed state, the Captain seemed to hear every sound with heightened clarity. The rumble of the engine, the slap and hiss of the river against the hull, the creak of timbers, the squeak of an ungreased bearing on the sternwheel and the voices of the men.

"Tryin' for the million dollar wound," Scott muttered sourly.

Although there was no longer any pain in his shoulder, Hedges imagined bolts of agony striking out from the older wounds in his right hip and left thigh. Sweat trickled over them and seemed to catch fire.

"What the friggin' use would that be to him in this neck of the woods?" Forrest snarled. "Come up and help me get him down, Billy. Scott, you take the wheel." He raised his voice to a bellow that beat painfully against Hedges' eardrums. "Rhett, come up here and watch from the bow. Bell, get to the stern. Rebs ain't gonna let us sail outta Richmond like we was pleasure cruising in New York habrour."

Footfalls clanged loudly on the iron sheeting of the citadel. But abruptly the noise receded, as though the men were running away from Hedges instead of towards him. At the same time, the sun seemed to be obscured by a dark cloud which cast a gigantic, advancing shadow across the countryside. Blood, he thought. A massive loss of blood through the bullet wound. Slowing his heart and starving his brain. That was what accounted for the illusion of heightened awareness. And now he was swamped by the after effect. The retreat of sound and advance of darkness were symptoms of oncoming unconsciousness. His one-handed grip on the wheel slipped loose and he crumpled to the deck of the pilothouse. The sweat seemed to freeze over his pores.

"The bastard don't look so goddamn tough now," somebody said from a great distance, shouting down a tunnel.

"Sleepin' like a baby, Frank. What say we blow a bigger hole in him and light out for Iowa right now?"

The farm was in Iowa. The farm being taken care of by Jamie with money Hedges sent home as regularly as the war allowed.

"You ever been to Iowa, Billy?"

"No, Frank."

"It covers a lot of area. Bigger than your mouth, even. Besides which, the longer this war lasts, the bigger our pay off."

"Some of us may not be alive to collect, Frank."

A wet spit, spattering against iron. Then a laugh. "Smaller the payroll, even bigger the pay off."

"You're too smart to be just a sergeant, Frank. I always said you ought to be an officer."

"Forget it, trooper," Forrest snarled, pulling rank. "I'm happy with the Captain here. He did okay busting us out. Maybe he's got some idea what the hell we do now."

"I hope he can think up somethin' fast. We'll be like sittin' ducks soon as they get us spotted."

"Looks of him, Hedges won't be doin' anythin' fast for awhile."

The injured Captain had been hovering on the brink of unconsciousness for a long time, hearing the words but unable to make sense of them or to atribute them to the speakers, whom he knew so well. Then, as the pit of total unawareness opened up for him and he began to tumble down, the words became crystal clear. But only for a moment, before they were driven deep into the recesses of his subconscious. Forrest's final remark seemed to hammer their evil meaning too far out of the reach of understanding.

"So let's help him get the lead out."

THE coffee had been good and the acrid sting of the cigarette smoke on his tongue heightened the pleasure of the aftertaste. He had made camp after two hours of easy riding from execution rock, in a small hollow at the side of a stream which probably fed the Columbia River tributary flowing past Paradise.

It was a good place for a man not in a hurry to rest himself and his horse. A high stand of timber shaded the hollow from the direct heat of the sun, there was ample brush for a fire, good grazing for the stallion and clear flowing water to refresh a weary body. First the half-breed had attended to his horse, then he had lit a fire and set the coffee pot to boil. Next, he had stripped the dusty, sweat-stiffened clothing from his hard, lean, sun-burnished body and stretched out naked in the shallow coolness of the stream until the coffee pot began to steam aromatically. He had dried himself with a blanket from his bedroll, dressed, drank two mugs of coffee and found enough tobacco in his keep to roll a single cigarette.

Throughout all this, his hooded blue eyes kept a constant surveillance over his surroundings and the cocked Winchester was never more than an arm's length away from him. That he could remain alert for a sign of danger threatening from any direction was the most important factor in his choice of the campsite. It was what he always sought first. Resting, eating, drinking, bathing and comforts for his horse were luxuries for a man like Edge when stacked against the need to survive. And the need to survive—to be constantly on his guard—had become a necessity to the half-breed. Too many men had a real or imagined reason to kill him, so that he could never completely relax, even in such an idyllic setting as this one.

But it was not the impassive, cool blue eyes peering out through a drifting screen of grey cigarette smoke that picked up the first danger signal. It was his ears, attuned to the regular noises of his surroundings, which detected an intrusion of strange sound, marking the approach of a rider.

"Steady, feller," he murmured to his horse as the stallion pricked his ears and stared nervously into the trees.

The stand of timber was the hollow's defensive weakness. To the west, north and south there was an arc of open terrain at least two hundred feet across at its narrowest. A small army of men could reach the timber fringe, fifty feet away, without being seen. But with the half-breed fully alert, they would have to be very quiet.

Edge flicked the cigarette butt into the stream, raised his knees and lifted the Winchester. He rested the barrel across the small vee between his kneecaps and curled a finger around the trigger. A lone rider, he guessed. Still quite deep in the timber and not paying particular heed to the need for silent progress. He aimed the rifle at the spot where he expected the rider to break into the open. But several times he had to readjust the aim as the rider veered to left and right, seeking the easiest path through the thickly growing trees. Edge had ample opportunity to glance often in other directions, checking that the rider in the timber was not a decoy. The hot spring sun continued to shed its bright light over an empty and unmoving land.

"Thank you, Lord," Angel Sarah said with a sigh as she steered a piebald gelding out of the trees.

She was offering gratitude for having found a way out of the timber. Her green eyes were tightly closed, her sweat-run face turned up to the sky and her hands clasped in prayer at her breasts. Edge elevated the aim of the rifle, bent his head low to sight and squeezed the trigger. The bullet drilled through the woman's poke bonnet with enough velocity to skim the hat from her head. Long, blonde hair tumbled out to frame the mask of terror which had gripped her features. Her mouth gaped to utter a scream, but fear constricted her throat, silencing the sound.

"Unless you brought my bankroll, lady, you got nothing to thank Him for," Edge said softly, levering another shell into the breech. He altered the cant of the rifle, drawing a bead just to the right of her clasped hands.

Her eyes seemed as wide as her mouth, the bright green of each pupil surrounded by an ocean of pure white. Then they snapped closed, her hands fell apart and she toppled sideways from the gelding. The well-schooled horse remained absolutely still as the woman thudded to the ground beside it.

Edge sighed and stood up, eyes raking the tree line and ears straining for another sound against the cheerful babbling of the stream. Then, certain Sarah was alone, he ambled up out of the hollow towards her. At first, he ignored her inert form, concentrating on the saddlebags. Both of them were empty. There was no canteen hanging from the horn and no bedroll strapped to the cantle. Making absolutely certain, he unbuckled the cinch and pushed the saddle off the gelding's back. No money fluttered out from underneath. As a final resort, before turning his attention to the senseless woman, he moved to where her bonnet had fallen and checked inside it. It was empty except for a faint, stimulating scent of female. He went back to the woman, straightened and rolled her into a supine position and raked his eyes over the high-necked, long-hemmed black dress. There were no pockets or pouches.

He crouched down beside her and hit her hard, back-handed, across the cheek. The blow flung her head to the side and left a vivid red mark on her wan skin. She made no sound and continued to breathe steadily. He pondered a moment, then withdrew the razor from the neck pouch. Because of the sideways twist of her head her jaw was no obstacle as he inserted the blade into the neck of the dress, honed edge against the serge. A thousand woven threads parting made a continuous, pleasant sound as he dragged the razor down the length of her body and legs. Sometimes it snagged on undergarments, but the keenness of the blade met the challenge with ease.

His expression impassive, he put away the razor, moved to the other side of the woman and crouched again. He gripped one half of the sliced dress and jerked it, standing upright at the same moment. She was slender and might have been weightless, so easily was the lean half-breed able to lift her. Her inert form came clear of the ground before her arms slid out of the dress sleeves. Then she fell hard to the ground dipping down into the hollow and began to roll. Naked except for a pair of scanty and now tattered pantaloons, she rolled over and over down the grassy bank: blonde hair flying, arms and legs flailing and small breasts bouncing. She did not scream until she plunged into the reviving water of the stream. By which time Edge had checked the inside of the dress and the under-garments for secret pockets. There were none.

His cool eyes surveyed Sarah's nakedness for the first time. She was sitting upright in the stream, spitting out water and gasping for breath. It took her several moments to return to full awareness. Moments during which the brown-crested breasts jutted in full exposure and the blonde triangle at the base of her flat belly was magnified by the clear water. Then she screamed again. In horror instead of alarm, as she clasped the tattered undergarment across her belly and thrust a forearm in front of her breasts.

"Dear Lord, what have you done?" she shrieked, the flush beginning at her face and rapidly spreading to diffuse colour over her entire marble-smooth body.

Edge dropped the ruined clothing, picked up the Winchester and met her shocked gaze with a bland one. "It's all right, ma'am," he said softly. "You took a tumble from your horse is all. Doesn't make you a fallen angel. Where's my money?"

"But I'm naked!"

"All you lost was your clothes. I'm the one that got screwed—out of more than a thousand bucks." He started down the slope. "Where is it?"

The sun was behind the half-breed and she squinted up at his tallness as he approached: there was no free hand to shade her eyes. Vulnerably naked, with the shoulder-length blonde hair framing her screwed-up face, and the water rushing around her, Angel Sarah was stunningly, erotically attractive.

"Please don't hurt me that way?" she pleaded as his shadow fell across her. "I'll tell you. It's why I came to find you. Please don't hurt me that way?"

He squatted down on the bank of the stream and sighed as he pointed the Winchester at her. "I'll allow I've been a long time from the well, but I reckon I can hold until there's something more satisfying than holy water," he told her softly. "And right now, I've got a more urgent need to fill—the space in my hip pocket where my bankroll used to be. That space has been aching like a pulled tooth ever since I made camp here. Stripped off to take a bath and found I'd already been taken to the cleaners."

"Look, I came to——"

"Shut your mouth, ma'am," he said in the same even tone. "Except to answer the questions. Where's my money?"

She swallowed hard. "Paradise. I came to——"

The half-breed canted the rifle and squeezed the trigger. Sarah screamed. The bullet hissed through the water between her splayed legs. It hit the bed of the stream and kicked mud up over her belly. He levered another shell into the breech and sighed.

"I'm angry, ma'am," he said. "Only two things make me really mad. Folks pointing guns at me and folks stealing from me. Just answer the questions. Where in Paradise?"

"With the cathedral fund," she replied hurriedly, her wide green eyes searching his face and figure for a sign of the anger he spoke of. But he seemed totally at ease; perhaps a little bored. "In the house of Arch Angel Luke."

"Who picked my pocket?"

"I don't——"

The Winchester cracked again. She didn't scream this time. But her naked flesh quivered in an uncontrollable fit of trembling as the bullet dove into the water, fractionally missing her flesh.

"Reckon you do."

"Angel Francis!" she shrieked, dropping both hands into the water to cover the hirsuite centre of her body. The dark brown nipples of her jutting, unfettered breasts were distended by fear. "In the store, after you'd paid for the supplies. While they were taking the body of Angel Angus out."

Edge gave a curt nod, then curled back his thin lips to show his teeth in a cold grin. The blue slits of his narrowed eyes were colder as they stared arrogantly at her exposed upper body. The flesh, almost transparently white again, continued to ripple with her fear.

"Always better to make a clean breast of things, ma'am," he said as he straightened. Then he touched his hat and turned away. He began to gather his gear together and saddle the stallion.

The woman remained silent for long moments, sitting in the gurgling water of the stream, struggling to bring the trembling under control.

"May I talk now?" she asked at length.

"All you like," he answered, not turning from his chores.

"I was the only one to get away from Paradise. Everybody else is still there. The lucky ones are dead. Those two white sinners and the indians . . . they are doing unspeakable things. I saw it. I came to ask your help."

"Is Francis dead?" Edge asked as he straightened from tightening the cinch.

"I don't know. I didn't stay to watch for long. They are torturing—for revenge and for the money . . . " Her voice trailed off. Then: "Oh, dear Lord!" she exclaimed. "If Angel Francis isn't . . . you'll kill him!"

Edge kicked dirt into the embers of the fire and swung up into the saddle. "I'm sure gonna do more than clip his wings, ma'am," he said softly.

The woman struggled upright and staggered out of the stream, unmindful of her total nudity as the remnants of her underwear dropped away. She fell to her knees beside the mounted half-breed and leaned back, spreading her arms in an attitude of wanton submission.

"Please?" she begged. "I came to ask for your help. Not for nothing. To tell you there is twenty-five thousand dollars in the cathedral fund. It's all yours if you'll rid our town of the sinners. But please—do not return to Paradise to kill Angel Francis. Please, I beg you. Take me. Take my body. Do whatever you want with me. But spare him."

The half-breed had not shaved in three days. The bristles made an ugly rasping sound as he dragged the back of his hand across his jaw. He eyed the arched body of the woman, the swells and indentations of her pale flesh running with sun-sparkling beads of stream water. Abruptly, she trembled again. But it was short and sharp and he knew from the way her lips parted and her eyes took on a misty sheen that it was not a spasm of fear this time. He recalled the appraising glances the woman had given him back in town and realised she was tremulously excited: uncontrollably aroused as she committed herself to sexual fulfilment after long years of disciplined frustration.

"Please, give me your answer," she begged, her voice a hoarse whisper.

"You've got a deal——"

A sound that was half a laugh, half a sob, choked from her throat. Her body sagged and then she fell back, splaying her naked thighs wide apart. Her breasts flattened, and rose and fell rapidly with her gasp-like breathing.

"On the money," the half-breed continued, surveying the submissive body coolly. "But not on the other."

"You . . . you . . . you . . . beast!" Sarah screamed at him as she struggled to her feet. She glared at him, her fury as naked as her body. "Don't you have any feelings?"

"Sure do, ma'am," Edge replied easily, as unmoved by her anger as he had been by her passion. "Right now I've got an urge to kill a man and an itch to collect twenty-five grand."

The softly spoken words penetrated the confusion of lust and rage clouding her mind. And she suddenly recalled her reason for seeking out Edge. She looked down at her nakedness, hoping it had all been a ghastly daydream. Then she gave a shriek of horror and scampered to snatch up her mutilated clothing. She held the razor-slashed gown and undergarments in front of her. Above the drab black of the material, her blonde hair framed a face that was vivid crimson.

"Dear Lord, how horrible!" she gasped with a tremor of revulsion. "Did it really happen?"

The half-breed clucked the stallion forward, heading him towards the trees. "Just like you remember it," he told her.

She shook her head, as if to clear it. Then she hastily discarded the tattered underwear and shrugged into the dress, coat-fashion, clutching it with her hands at waist and breasts. She ran awkwardly for her horse.

"Wait, I'm coming!" she called after the half-breed as he steered the stallion into the timber.

His tone was sardonic as the words emerged from the trees: "Figured you would after all that hard breathing."

CHAPTER SIX

THERE were no frigates lurking on the far side of the bluff around the bend in the river. The *Southern Glory* with John Scott at the wheel churned through the morning brightness unmolested, putting Richmond further behind her with each turn of the big sternwheel. The trooper enjoyed the novelty of steering the slow-moving ironclad along the sun-sparkling river with the pleasant, peaceful countryside of Virginia spread out on either side. He yawned a great deal.

Standing their watches at bow and stern, Rhett and Bell felt the tensions of the past few days, climaxed by the blood run out of Richmond, ebb from their weary bodies as they basked in the warm sunlight. Their eyelids drooped.

In the engine room, Douglas had come to realise that the old-timer could be trusted as long as he was allowed to relive his past. The heat from the furnace hastened the corporal's drowsiness.

Inside the citadel, Myron watched with hollow eyes as Forrest used the razor to prise the bullet from Hedges' shoulder. Seward watched the Rebel deserter. The Captain remained unconscious.

"Ricochet," Forrest said pensively as he examined the misshapen bullet, rolling it between a bloodied thumb and finger. "Didn't have enough speed left to go in deep. Made a mess of a few veins which is why the bastard bled like a stuck pig.

"Maybe the mortification will set in and the bastard'll die," Myron muttered dully.

Forrest used the slight flexibility of the razor's blade to flick the bullet across the citadel deck. Then he indicated the medical supplies chest which had been found in a locker. "Pour some antiseptic in the hole and bandage him up, Billy," he instructed wearily. "Somethin' I gotta do."

Seward went to the chore reluctantly and far from gently. A high scream of pain from Myron interrupted him. He whirled and his youthful face was suddenly split by a grin. Myron had been squatting on his haunches, but a vicious kick from Forrest had sent him sprawling out, flat on his back. The damaging boot was now pressing down on his throat, trapping him. The sergeant, his face contorted by a snarl, stooped down, brandishing the razor in front of Myron's terrified eyes.

"You said something bad about our poor, wounded Captain," Forrest rasped.

"Jesus, you been cursin' him ever since you started diggin' out the bullet," Myron protested, his voice squeaky with pain.

"But I ain't a Reb, Reb," the sergeant countered. "Makes a difference."

"He killed my brother! He killed Floyd!"

"He makes mistakes sometimes." Forrest had moderated his voice to a tone of mock regret. "One day one of them is going to get him killed. But not today. Because the mistake of only killing one Reb when he could have killed two lets me have a crack of the whip—so to speak."

"Please, sergeant?" Myron forced around the solid lump of fear that had risen into his already constricted throat.

"Fresh out of favours, Reb," Forrest said evenly. "All I got left is unkind cuts."

Myron screamed again and screwed his eyes tight shut as the blade plunged towards him. The steel point pierced his eyelid, penetrated the ball and then, by a flick of Forrest's wrist, was angled into his brain. The emaciated body twitched once as the nerves spasmed into death. Then Myron lay utterly still.

"Terrific, Frank!" Seward gasped as Forrest straightened up, wiping the blood from the razor on his pants leg. "What did it feel like, pushing the blade in him."

The sergeant spat on to the dead body. "What did it feel like when you put a mortar shell into those Rebs on the dock, Billy?"

"Good, Frank. Real good." Grinning at the memory, Seward

turned to finish dressing Hedges' wound. The good humour evaporated and he swallowed hard.

The Captain was sitting up, hooded eyes flicking from the bloodied-faced dead man to the scowling Forrest. "And blasting cannon shells into a stone wall didn't have the same charge, uh, sergeant?" he said softly. His face was still deathly pale beneath the heavy stubble.

Forrest seemed near hurling an angry retort, but brought himself under control. He ambled over to where Hedges sat and handed him the razor. "I joined this man's army to kill the enemy, sir," he replied. "He was a yellow-belly Johnnie Reb figurin' to get brave on account of what you done to his brother. He was the enemy and it was gettin' to be a long time since I killed any like him."

Rhett pushed his head through one of the gun ports at the forward end of the citadel. "Won't be so long before you get another chance, Frank!" he called, a tremor of nervousness in his voice. "There's a frigging great steamship heading for us."

"You want me to handle it, Captain?" Forrest asked.

Hedges wiped the razor again, ensuring every trace of blood was off the blade, and thrust it into the pouch. Then he hauled himself to his feet, using Seward for support. "Check the situation, sergeant," he ordered tersely. "I'll be on deck as soon as I'm patched up."

He turned his back on Seward, presenting the wound to him for attention. Forrest grunted, picked up his Spencer from where it leaned against a stores bin and headed for the hatchway to the outer deck. Seward had already treated the bullet wound with antiseptic. Now he applied a dressing pad and began to wind bandage around the injured shoulder.

"The Reb was makin' threatenin' noises, Captain," the trooper explained. "If one of us didn't get him, he'd have creamed you first chance he got, that's for sure."

"It's a great comfort to know I'm surrounded by men who take such care of me," Hedges rasped, gingerly pulling on his bloodstained shirt after the bandage was tied.

"Billy, get up here soon as you can!" Forrest yelled. "Bell and

Rhett, get out of sight, for Christ sake. This is supposed to be a Reb navy tub! You look like friggin' hobos!"

Seward grinned, "Sounds like slippin' it to Myron did Frank a power of good, sir. He's his old self again."

"Yeah, surprising how a quick killing enriches a man," Hedges replied softly as Rhett and Bell squeezed into the citadel through gun ports. "He gave you an order, trooper."

"Yes, sir!" Seward snapped, grabbing his rifle and doubling out through the hatchway.

Hedges trailed him, more slowly, careful to keep his upper body still, for the slightest movement set off a fireball of pain in the injured shoulder. Before he stepped out into the bright sunlight he was sweating from the effort of forcing one weak step after another. He went down on one knee in the angle between the aft bulkhead of the citadel and the smokestack. From this position he could survey the river ahead, rest, and be in reasonable cover.

The ship ploughing upriver towards the *Southern Glory* was still some way off. A mile at least. But close enough to be recognised as a powered clipper. Her sails were furled and black wood smoke wafted from her aft-mounted smokestack.

"What you reckon, Frank?" John Scott called back.

He and Seward had stationed themselves forward of the citadel and held their Spencers canted across the front of their bodies. The copy Colts jutted from the waistbands of their uniform pants. They were close enough to the forward gunports to duck into the cover of the armour plating if it proved necessary.

"Wait for the friggin' order, trooper!" Forrest roared in his rank-pulling voice. Then he leaned through a side port in the pilothouse. There was a red indentation around his right eye from where he had held the telescope pressed tight against his flesh. "I figure they got river defences someplace up ahead, Captain," he said calmly. "Forts, maybe. That's why they ain't come after us or brought up some artillery pieces to blast us."

"Been kind of quiet," Hedges agreed. "What d'you read through the eyeglass, sergeant?"

"Cargo vessel, sir. Flying the British flag. Blockade runner. Armed with the same kind of guns we got. Looks quiet. Like they don't expect us to be anything 'cepting a Reb ironclad makin' for sea."

"So let's give them a surprise," Hedges said. "If you're still in the mood, sergeant?"

"What do you think, Captain?" Forrest answered, splitting his lips for a grin. "Myron was just an appetite whetter, like they say. I'm about ready for a decent meal."

"You're a glutton for other men's punishment, sergeant." He returned the grin and at once re-established the familiar rapport that existed under battle conditions. "Whistle Douglas up into the citadel and tell the old man to keep stoking." He raised his voice. "You troopers forward—inside."

"Move it!" Forrest roared, letting every man within earshot know that he was with the Captain all the way—and that they had better be likewise.

"Anything special you want me to do?" the sergeant asked as Hedges ducked in through the hatchway.

"Just be ready to abandon ship damn fast," Hedges answered.

"You mean jump over the side and start walkin'?" Forrest yelled.

"You're only a cavalry sergeant," Hedges called. "You ain't got that much pull. Just swim like hell, or get blasted there."

EDGE inched out on to execution rock, sliding along on his belly. Behind him, Angel Sarah used one hand to hold the dress together and with the other kept a tight grip on the reins of the two horses. She was well back from the rock overhang, safe from being skylined.

"What did they burn?" she rasped in a harsh whisper.

They had seen the pall of black smoke from several miles off—an ominous sign against the blue sky which marked the location of the valley. As they drew nearer, the smoke disintegrated as the fire burned out. But the smell of it was strong in their nostrils all the way to the crest of the valley's western slope. Now, as Edge stretched out on the rocky vantage point, he saw the blackened remains of the field fire, no longer wisping with smoke but still emanating the dry, musky scent of charred crops.

"The fields," he answered, taking in at a single glance the entire fire-razed area from the river to the edge of the town. "Slaughtered the beef, too. Cathedral got a little sooted up."

Then his nostrils picked up another odour that was more cloying. A little from the dead cows, he guessed. But mostly from the bodies of the townspeople who had been left in the fields where they fell.

"The people?" she asked in a hoarse whisper, fearful of the answer. "The Earthly Angels?"

Edge had inched forward and was staring directly down upon the town, now in patchy shadow as the afternoon sun dipped behind the trees at the top of the valley slope. The scene was horrifying, but the clear blue eyes of the half-breed surveyed the tableau of human suffering with the same unemotional expression as when he had looked at the burned fields.

"Maybe fifteen or twenty have got their wings," he reported as he wriggled back off the rock and stood up. "Too far off to see whether Francis is one of the high fliers." He took the reins of the stallion from her and swung into the saddle.

"I'm praying that you may pull back from the brink of murder of Angel Francis," she said earnestly as she mounted the gelding.

"But blasting the trappers and the indians is okay, uh?" He moved towards the downward path by which he had left Paradise earlier.

"An eye for an eye," Angel Sarah countered. "They are murderers themselves."

"And it's the Lord's will," he boomed in imitation of Arch Angel Luke's sermonizing tones.

"You are right, but I fear you mock, sinner."

The woman's voice and attitude had changed, reverting to the stylised speech and earnestness that was common to the Earthly Angels. The naked woman, begging to be taken, back at the hollow could have been another person. It was as if the return to Paradise had a physical and emotional influence on her.

Two more Earthly Angels died as Edge steered the stallion down through the trees. They died hard, like the others before them: with high, thin, tremulous screams of agony that rose up the valley side and silenced the sounds of nature in the timber. Riding behind the half-breed, the woman became rigidly tense at each audible sign of suffering. But she said nothing, aware that Edge had his own good reasons for wanting to reach the town: that he was negotiating the steeply sloping ground as fast as was possible.

Just once, as they drew near to the cemetery in the grove, she interrupted a short space of calm between a dying scream and a burst of insane laughter. "All indians are savages!" she hissed with low venom.

"Just a different colour is all," Edge muttered in reply, recalling a montage of savagery from the past: of brutal atrocities committed by men of many colours and creeds. One of the meanest killers he had known was a Quaker.*

He reined the stallion to a halt at the fringes of the grove, dismounted and hitched the animal to a tree.

"I will accompany you all the way," the woman announced firmly as she dismounted and Edge slid the Winchester from the boot.

He loaded three shells to make up for those fired at the hollow. "I was counting on it," he told her. "I may need a diversion."

The spring air was chill where the sun did not reach, but not as cold as the tall, lean half-breed as he skirted the marker-featured grove to reach the town side. He was like a stalking animal, still carrying a hard ball of anger inside him, but controlling it. Early in his violent life he had learned that the heat of anger powers desire but ruins performance. Coldly, he had killed many men whose judgments were clouded by hot ire.

"Dear Lord, we have sinned much to merit this retribution," the woman murmured, her words no louder than the breaking of grass blades beneath their feet as they crouched at the edge of the punishment area.

Although he was within a few yards of where the dead lay,

**See—Edge: Blood on Silver.*

Edge was still unable to see whether Francis was amongst them, or to make an accurate estimate of how many there were. For they were piled in a ghastly heap of naked, blood-run white flesh at the rear of the area. And even as he watched, peering through a patch of brush and between the splayed legs of a swaying indian, another limp, naked form was released from the pillory and flung on to the charnal pile.

He heard a faint rustling sound behind him and swung his head round. But it was only the woman crawling away, struggling to control her nausea until she could find a place to throw up in safety. The half-breed turned his impassive eyes back to the torture scene as a woman screamed and men laughed. The loudest sounds of mirth came from Gabb and Mackinlay who were sprawled on the ground in front of the house at the top of the street. Each had a bottle of whiskey in one hand, and an arm around the naked body of a terrified woman. Gabb had claimed the younger Edith, who was as nubile and statuesque as Sarah. Mackinlay was cupping the sagging breast of a much older woman. The white men's faces were contorted and coloured by liquor. The women's fear-twisted features and pathetically exposed bodies were bruised and scratched.

The scream had come from another woman of perhaps sixty-five. She had been dragged from the barn by two bottle-toting indians who hauled her along the roughened street by her wrists. The laughter had erupted from the white men and the other drunken Spokans as the old woman's captors began to run—too fast for the captive to remain erect. When she was flung down in front of the pillory, her dress had been torn to shreds on the street. Two more indians dashed forward with whoops of delight, brandishing knives. The clothing was slashed from the frail, wrinkled body. Blood splashed from beneath the honed edges and points of carelessly-wielded blades.

The old woman was praying and sobbing as she was forced upright. Her neck and wrists were fitted into the cut-outs in the pillory and the hinged top was slammed down. The excited laughter faultered and faded. Raddle-faced indians sucked from bottles. Gabb and Mackinlay drank one-handed while the fingers of their other hands roved across female flesh, probing and kneading: drawing moans of pain from the women they had claimed. The old woman had no more prayers to offer and her trapped body shook with sobs. A knife hissed through the chill air, then another. A thud . . . a scream . . . another thud . . . another scream. The knarled, bony hands of the prisoner had hung limply in front of the pillory board. Suddenly they were pinned there, the quivering hilts of the knives seeming to grow from their backs. Blood trickled down the stiffened fingers.

A drunken indian dropped his breechcloth, took a final swig from his bottle and then moved towards the woman from the back. His readiness was cheered by the glittering-eyed watchers as he reeled and steadied himself. Another indian approached the woman from the front, drawing a knife and clutching a handful of her thin white hair. The knife point was pressed against her pulsing throat.

Edge drew back from the fringe of the punishment area. He stood up, turned and looked into the gaunt, hollow-eyed face of Angel Sarah. Yellow, brown and red signs of her nausea were caking on her jaw. The cheering rose in raucous volume, then subsided to gasps of release, punctuated by hoarse-voiced obscenities as Gabb encouraged the two Spokans in their assault.

"Has there ever been anything more vile?" Sarah hissed.

"The Apaches and the Sioux know a few tricks they could teach this bunch," Edge muttered, moving away down the slope behind the row of houses on the barn side of the street.

Uppermost in his mind, flashed the Sioux uprising in which his wife had died. But there had been other run-ins with Indians—both Sioux* and the even more cruel Apaches.†

Sarah crept along at his heels, uncaring about the slit dress anymore. It gaped wide, exposing her from neck to thighs as she held the low skirt hem clear of her feet to avoid tripping.

She halted and crouched down beside the apparently relaxed half-breed at one corner of the barn. From inside came the low murmurings of many voices engaged in ardent, soft-voiced

**See—Edge: Bloody Summer.*
†See—Edge: Apache Death.

prayer. Far off, from the punishment area at the top of the street, came the shrill sound of the old woman's dying scream. Sarah shuddered.

"What are you going to do?" she rasped, then followed the direction of the narrow-eyed gaze.

She saw the wagon, still with the team hitched, parked between the barn and the stable across the street. She read the faded sign on the side: OREGON MINING COMPANY. She saw the freight it carried, revealed now that the burlap cover had been folded back. Cases of rye whiskey, two of them broken open and almost empty. And crates, all firmly sealed, marked OREGON MINING COMPANY—BLASTING POWDER.

"May the Lord have mercy on the soul of departed Angel Amelia," Arch Angel Luke said loudly from within the barn.

"I see deliverence from this evil!" the high voice of Prophet Thomas proclaimed.

Edge glanced up at the window under which he and Sarah were crouched. The button nose of the round-faced little man was pressed against the pane, his tiny eyes gleaming. "I think that feller's a fake, ma'am," he said.

"What are you going to do?" the woman insisted as running feet thudded against the street.

"Lot of other people having fun," the half-breed murmured, eyeing the wagon again. "We might as well get a bang out of it."

CHAPTER SEVEN

RHETT went over the side of the ironclad first, his boots hung around his neck, kicking wildly to swim clear of the thrashing sternwheel. Then Douglas, Seward, Bell and Scott. Crouched behind the citadel at the side of the pilothouse, Hedges watched the five troopers move away from the *Southern Glory*; ensuring that they followed his orders and maintained a course which kept the bulk of the ironclad between themselves and the approaching clipper.

"Reckon we're close enough to start it now, sir," Forrest reported from above and Hedges swung around to look along the length of the boat.

The clipper loomed large off the starboard bow, keeping firmly in the upriver channel. Forrest, sweating and with lips drawn back, eyes gleaming, held the ironclad steadily on a passing course. The clipper was named *Stanstead* and she was running easily under power. Few of the crew members on deck had any duties to perform and they lounged idly against spars, deck cargo and unprimed cannon, watching the approach of the *Southern Glory*.

Sunlight bounced on the lens of a telescope and Hedges ducked below the level of the citadel, striking a match.

"Ahoy there, *Southern Glory*!" a British voice hailed, amplified by a bullhorn.

"Frig off, you lousy limey," Forrest muttered as the bows of the two vessels drew level, disturbed water clashing between them.

"What you got against the British, sergeant?" Hedges asked smoothly as he touched the match to the end of the powder fuse.

"Picked the wrong side, that's all," Forrest answered.

"Reason enough," the Captain allowed as he watched the sparking fire flare along the fuse. Then raised his eyes to peer through the gloom of the citadel to where the troopers had stacked cases of powder around the forward cannon. The bodies of Myron and the four Confedrate seamen were propped against the cases. Their dead eyes stared back at Hedges in mute accusation.

"Haven't you got a word of welcome for your allies?" the British ship's officer demanded, riled.

Grinning, Forrest spun the wheel, then jammed the telescope through the spokes and against the binnacle. The ironclad swung into a lazy turn to starboard: held on the arcing course by the firmly snagged wheel.

"How about goodbye!" the sergeant roared, lunging from the pilothouse and leaping to the citadel deck.

Cries of alarm and fear rang out from the British clipper. Sharp orders cut across the babble. The helmsman spun the wheel to try to sheer away from the collision. The telegraph clanged for full speed ahead. Seamen, jerked out of idleness, sprinted to reach their weapons. The fire hissed along the fuse, consuming fresh powder and leaving a snakelike trail of blackened remains behind it. The blunt prow of the *Southern Glory* closed for a midships collision with the *Stanstead.* A burst of rifle fire cracked. Bullets clanged against the ironclad's armour plating. The troopers in the water angled towards the river's northern bank.

Forrest hit the deck and bellied behind the pilothouse. He dragged out a wooden raft with the Spencers, Confederate Colts and cartons of ammunition lashed to it. "You can have that Captain last to leave his ship routine," he yelled above the crack, whine and clang of bullets.

He went over the side, hauling on a rope that splashed the raft into the water after him. Hedges was only a moment behind him, kicking out with his legs and reaching forward with his good arm to grip a rope trailing from the raft. Some of the troopers were already wading ashore, flinging themselves into the reeds as bullets whined towards them. With all need for subterfuge passed, Forrest struck out strongly for the bank. His strength was more than a match for his burdens over a short distance.

The prow of the ironclad crunched into the side of the clipper. The sound of splintering wood was almost swamped by the rumble of two engines and bedlam of shouting voices. Then the fire reached the climactic end of its snaking course. The roar of the explosion took the form of a deafening crack, the searing blast hammering the sound waves against the eardrums. For a split-second even the light of the sun seemed to dim as a mighty crimson and orange flame licked into the sky. Then a pall of dense, oil-black smoke billowed up around it. Debris was rocketed through the smoke, some of it comprised of the torn-apart sections of men, all of it blackened and dripping flames. As it rained down, the men on the bank dived low into the reeds. Those in the water forced themselves under. Then, as their ears recovered from the punishing blast of the first explosion, another burst from the holds of the clipper.

It was louder than the first, ripping the *Stanstead* in two, rearing the sections away and thrusting the sinking ironclad across the river. Flames shot sideways as well as skywards and unrecognisable pieces of ship and men were hurled in every direction.

"She must have been carrying explosives!" Bell yelled, pressing his face into the mud of the bank as the second blast-driven shower of debris pelted down all round.

"Sure enough wasn't no popcorn," Douglas muttered.

A blasted-off hand thudded into the reeds where Seward was sprawled. The index finger pointed accusingly at the youngster. "I just did what the officer told me, buddy," he said with a giggle. Enough of the flesh had been seared from the bones so that he was able to remove the two gold rings easily before tossing the hand into the water.

It bounced off Forrest's head as the sergeant surfaced, towing the raft. "What the hell?" he snarled.

"Figured you might need a hand," Seward giggled.

Forrest spat and staggered upright, dragging his feet through the silt of the riverbed as he waded into the reeds. The others rose, gathering around the raft to claim weapons. Hedges struggled through the reeds and flopped down wearily on the lush grass of the bank. His shoulder was throbbing and his ears still rang from the double explosion. He looked out over the river, now calm again. The sunlight was still dimmed by the dense cloud of black smoke which hung in the unmoving air. Nothing stirred on either of the wrecked ships except for tongues of flame in isolated pockets of fire. The front section of the ironclad had disintegrated and her no longer turning sternwheel hung in mid-air. She rested partly on the riverbed, as did both halves of the clipper.

"A rifle and a revolver, sir," Forrest said, thrusting the two guns towards Hedges. "I guess you didn't just forget about the old-timer in the engine room?"

"We had to have maximum speed to the end," the Captain answered. "At least he died happy."

He looked around at the troopers squatting on the bank. Now that the job was over, their weariness was creeping back. But it was encroaching more strongly now, taking toll of the long hours without sleep or food. Something akin to sheer exhaustion held their eyelids low, distorted their mouth lines and etched deep scores into the grimed skin beneath their stubble.

"Gotta admit I clean forgot about the old coot," Douglas confessed. "But you're right, sir. He was like a kid with his first whore, messing with that engine."

"Gave him a hot time," Scott said, thrusting the stock of his Spencer into the river.

Many bodies were drifting down river on the ebbing tide. The one he had trapped by hooking the rifle stock under the crotch was burnt to a cinder in human form. But the facial features were still recognisable, moulded in pitch black into the form of Robert Chivers' face. Minus the beard of course. Hedges eyed the grisly sight pensively, wondering if it was a smile of pleasure or grimace of agony that held the lips wide over toothless gums. He guessed the furnace had burst and spewed flaming fuel when the ironclad exploded.

"Damn shame," Douglas said. "Don't reckon he was happy." Then he guffawed. "Looks pretty burned up about it."

Hedges used the Spencer to help him to his feet. "There's a war on," he said. "We've all got to make sacrifices. Let's move out."

Seward eyed Forrest hopefully, searching for support in an argument against moving before the men had rested. But Forrest was tight-lipped and grim-faced. The youngster looked at the others and found them surveying their surroundings with the same scrutiny that Hedges and the sergeant had already shown. Safety lay to the north, beyond a wide area where danger might lurk at every turn. So it was in this direction that the tired eyes peered. Across swampy meadowland to a road. And then further, over fields of wheat ripening in the spring sunshine. Further still, to the distant hump of a hill. There was not a trace of human habitation for as far as the eye could see. But this very emptiness of the landscape presented an eerie prospect to the other troopers, which quickly infected Seward.

"I'm with you, sir," the youngster said enthusiastically, clutching his Spencer tightly as he rose. "Reckon every Reb within twenty miles of here heard us bust up their boats."

"You ain't a bright kid, Billy," Forrest rasped. "But just sometimes you show you've got an ounce of sense someplace in that lunkhead of yours."

Hedges led the way, swinging his injured arm gingerly to keep the circulation flowing. He set a fast walking pace across the springy turf and over the hard-packed dirt of the road. Then, in the wheat, growing tall enough to give them cover if they should need to dive to the ground, he slowed. The troopers were anxious to put distance between themselves and the scene of the river wreckage, but the Captain knew that neither the men nor himself could maintain a hot pace for long. Fear of mass pursuit, although a strong motivating factor, could not supplement flagging physical stamina. Exhaustion was an enemy equally as dangerous as Rebel troops.

"We're leavin' a trail a blind idiot could follow," Forest pointed out as they emerged from the wheat field, crossed a dry ditch and moved into barley. Behind them a path of trampled crops, two men wide, cut back arrow-straight to the road.

"Ain't blind idiots leaving it, sergeant," Hedges muttered, gritting his teeth as the constant movement of his arm kept the pain hot in his shoulder. "I can see a whole mess of cornfields that had to be ploughed and seeded and some time will have to be harvested."

"You sure ain't blind," Forrest allowed sarcastically.

Hedges ignored the sergeant's tone as he tramped into the barley. "So where's the damn farm buildings?" he asked softly.

Forrest grinned. "With food and horses?"

Hedges nooded. "I'm sure hungry. And I seem to remember being a cavalryman one time."

Ten minutes later he saw what he was searching for. The ground dipped suddenly, sloping away into a shallow basin that had not been visible from the river. The cultivated fields ended at a row of trees beyond which a grassy meadow stretched gently downwards. Sheep grazed peacefully on the turf in the foreground. Cows chewed the cud lower down.

"Lamb chops," Seward muttered with relish.

"Holy cow!" Rhett countered, licking his lips.

Beyond the feeding animals, set amid a grove of more trees, was a walled monastery. From their position on high ground, the weary troopers were able to see over the wall. Hooded monks, their habits trailing on the ground, glided across a large square of trimmed lawn, hands clasped in prayer. Two tended vegetable patch in a shaded corner. Another drew water from a well to fill a pitcher.

"You figure heaven's on our side, Captain?" Bell asked.

They had all instinctively sunk to the ground when they spotted the monastic retreat. Now, as the enlisted men eyed the prospect of food and rest with eager anticipation, Hedges and Forrest held aside prickly brush to survey the entire basin.

"Luck that we found it," Scott growled, suddenly infected by the mood of caution which had gripped the Captain and sergeant. "Good or bad?"

"One way to find out," Douglas muttered. "Will you look at those sweet little old potatoes that holy guy is diggin'."

"Corporal!" Hedges snapped.

It was too quiet—the peaceful calm of the monastery eerily out of context after the massive explosions which had thundered less than a mile away and no more than twenty minutes ago. And suddenly the off-key serenity was shattered. Douglas was out in the open, taking his first long stride across the turf, when Hedges' warning pulled him up short. The single word probably saved his life. But didn't prevent a bullet boring into his flesh and cracking his right forearm.

"Jesus Christ, the bastards!" he said in bewilderment as half a dozen other bullets whined past his head or spurted divots from the turf around him. Then he saw the blood streaming from the hole in his shirt sleeve. "I've been hit!" he screamed. Then he whirled and powered into a dive that crashed him back among the flattened troopers in the brush.

"Should have been in your friggin' head!" Forrest snarled at him, and sent a shot cracking towards the corner of the monastery wall from which the fusillade of rifle fire had come.

Hedges and Seward snapped off shots a moment later, the bullets whining across the backs of panicked sheep and cattle. All three shells dug chips of stone out of the wall angle.

"That ain't damn religious!" Seward rasped, levering a new round into the breach as he watched the monks within the walls scatter for cover. "Shootin' at people."

"Ain't the holy men blasted at us," Forrest muttered.

"Not unless there's an order got the same grey threads and brass buttons as Rebel infantry," Hedges supplemented, drawing a bead on the wall angle again. A rifle barrel was thrust into sight. A head followed it.

Forrest and Hedges fired in unison. The pale flesh of the Rebel's face was pitted by two ugly holes. Crimson splashed a pair of zig-zag lines across the green turf. The Rebel reeled backwards, out of sight.

"Don't give a shit who done it!" Douglas whined. "I got hit!" He groaned. "Help me, somebody?"

"Billy?" Forrest said.

"Yeah, Frank?"

"All that noise Hal's makin' is gettin' to be irksome. Give him a hand, uh?"

"How, Frank?"

"Across the friggin' mouth!"

Seward lashed out, but Douglas rolled out of range.

"Okay, okay!" the corporal whined.

"Must have been patrolling around here when the boats blew," Forrest said to Hedges. "Saw us heading north and this is the only cover in the area."

"Past doesn't matter," Rhett moaned, clutching his Spencer tightly to keep his hands from trembling. "They aren't going to just keep sticking out their heads to be shot off."

The sergeant spat. "Real wise, trooper," he said wryly. "That high price education of yours tell you what we ought to do now?"

"All I know is we should thank Corporal Douglas. We'd all have been shot if he didn't show himself."

"Friggin' right," Douglas rasped through gritted teeth.

"And the Rebs wouldn't know where we were if he didn't take his mornin' stroll," Scott countered grimly.

"Damn right," Forrest said quickly, grasping at a way out of the verbal battle he looked like losing.

Hedges heard the exchanges without listening to them: his narrowed eyes raking the four hundred feet of sloping turf between where he lay and the rearing wall of the monastery. Sheep and cattle continued to roam the area, still skittish but no longer galloping in panic now that the firing had stopped. On the other side of the wall, the monastery appeared deserted, every monk having scuttled clear of the lawned quadrangle to seek cover. The splashes of blood on the grass formed a bright marker pointing to the position where the Rebel soldiers waited. If they were still there. The built-up tensions of the long wait had caused them to blunder, announcing their presence before all seven troopers were in sight. But there was no guarantee they would continue to play it wrong and stay in the same position. The wall angle diagonally across the quadrangle from where they had fired offered another area of solid cover within sight of the troopers. And, if there was a door other than the main one which faced up the slope, the Rebels could have infiltrated the monastery.

"I don't reckon no charge down the hill, sir," the sergeant said when he saw that Hedges had completed the new survey. "On the run we'd lose accuracy and the Rebs'd be able to pick us off like crippled jack rabbits."

"And no good trying to flank the bastards," Bell put in. "Open terrain no matter which way we hit."

"And they gotta figure we might try it," Scott said.

"They don't seem in any hurry to start the shooting again." This from Rhett, less tense now that several minutes had past without gunfire shattering the tranquility of the verdant basin.

"Like they're waitin' for somethin'," Douglas rasped.

"May have sent a man for reinforcements when they saw us come outta the river," the sergeant suggested, and grinned. "Heard about our rep. Know it takes more than a handful of Rebs to handle this Union troop."

"Oh, Christ!" Rhett gasped. "Let's circle wide and take off."

"Well, Captain?" Forrest wanted to know, meeting the blue slits of Hedges eyes with a level, challenging stare.

"Can't make an omelette without cracking eggs, sergeant," the Captain said softly. "Or mutton stew without killing the meat."

Forrest was angrily puzzled for a moment, then a grin spread across his grizzled face. "Got a preference for beef myself, sir."

Both men turned to look down the slope, drawing beads with their Spencers. The rifles cracked and animals were taken on the run and keeled over. The lever actions were worked, spinning the ejected cartridges into the brush. Spooked by the first shots, the sheep and cattle raced and turned, colliding with each other. The Spencers exploded more sound.

Giggling, Billy Seward joined in the slaughter.

"We ain't that hungry," Rhett muttered into a moment of silence between shots, gazing ruefully at the mounting number of animals carcasses littering the slope.

"Ain't all for eatin', you New England dude!" Bell yelled

starting to fire as he realised the reason for the slaughter. "Them dead animals are our cover for making it down the slope."

"Well I'll be buggered!" Rhett exclaimed.

"Don't he get the urge at the strangest times?" Bell yelled as he drilled a bullet into the brain of a panicked cow.

THE two Spokan indians burst through the entrance to the church section of the barn. One of them levelled a Winchester while the other sprinted into the huddle of terrified Earthly Angels. A frail old man was dragged from the group.

"It is the will of the Lord!" Arch Angel Luke boomed after the retreating indians and their struggling captive. "We shall pray for your soul, Angel Joseph."

His hat pushed on to the back of his head, Edge shot a glance around the corner of the barn. He peered along the street for only a split-second, but it was enough. The black-garbed victim was being forced to run up the slope towards the punishment area. The waiting indians watched in eager anticipation. But Gabb and Mackinlay had had their fill of spectator sport for awhile. They had risen from in front of the house and were dragging their naked women down the incline of the street. Lust and alcohol coloured and contorted the faces of the trappers. For the first time, Edge noticed the ugly yellow fester covering the untreated bullet wound on the back of Gabb's right hand. But he was apparently immune to pain as he raised the hand to tilt the bottle to his lips. Then he hurled the bottle away from him and turned abruptly to shove the terrified Edith through an open doorway. Mackinlay scooped up his woman and laughed hysterically as he carried her into the same house.

The half-breed could no longer see what was happening, but a roar of approval from the punishment area signalled that the angel named Joseph had reached his place of brutal execution. The double doors at the end of the barn were fastened with a length of timber slotted through two brackets.

"How'd you raise twenty-five thousand dollars?" he asked as he lifted the bar.

"Some of us were rich when we were sinners," the white-faced Sarah answered. "Most of it was donated by myself and the other Earthly Angels. The balance we earned working in the fields."

"And picking pockets," Edge added as he opened the doors.

"Some sinners paid their fines without resort to such things," the woman answered flatly. "According to the will——"

"Of the Lord . . . I know," Edge cut in and quickly raked his eyes over the shocked faces of the Earthly Angels who stared back at him from inside the barn. They had moved from the church section in response to the urgings of Prophet Thomas and were huddled in a tight-knit group. His narrowed eyes failed to spot Francis.

"All events are thus pre-ordained," Sarah said dully as the captive at the top of the street shrilled his first scream. "It is why the Earthly Angels do not resist."

"Lord helps them that helps themselves," the half-breed rasped, turning away from the barn entrance. "I work for money. And I ain't getting paid for carrying them out of there."

He went to the corner of the barn and checked the street. It was empty. Every eye on the punishment area was directed towards the white man held prisoner in the stocks. His screams were coming faster and louder now, as two drunken Spokans carved off his toes. Lustful laughter and agonised groans came from the house into which Gabb and Mackinlay had taken their women. He reached the wagon in three long strides and climbed up on to the seat. The smooth wood was spitted by bullet holes and stained with old blood from the time it had been stolen. As he softly coaxed the team into a turn, Sarah convinced the towns-people to leave the barn. He could hear her arguing that it was the Lord's will she should escape the attack, find Edge and bring him back. She didn't say anything about money.

"We beg forgiveness for regarding you unkindly, sinner," Arch Angel Luke proclaimed. "We ask that you——"

"Don't ask anything else, feller," Edge rasped as he jumped from the seat and began to back up the horses, reversing the wagon in through the gaping doorway. "You can't afford it."

Sarah, holding the tattered dress tightly around her body now, had joined the group of some fifty survivors who were clustered behind the barn. The white-haired man had taken a position at their head.

"The Lord has sent you, sinner," he said in the same unwavering tone. "We place ourselves in your hands."

"Just get out of my hair," Edge told him. "Take them into the trees someplace."

"So be it," Luke replied, and turned away to lead his followers at an unhurried pace.

"Not you!" Edge snapped, reaching out to jerk Sarah from the group. "Stick around."

She complied with cold resignation.

Edge watched the black-garbed group for a moment, then climbed up and over the wagon to check the street again. At the top end, Joseph's tortured feet dripped blood in front of the stocks. But he was no longer screaming. An indian was forcing whiskey down his throat, trying to revive him from merciful unconsciousness.

"Wake up and keep them happy for a while longer, feller," the half-breed murmured, whirling to clamber over the wagon again.

"What am I to do?" Sarah wanted to know.

The half-breed watched the back markers of the escaping group go from sight among the trees. Then he reached out, hooked his long fingers and gripped the high neck of her dress. "Turn around and let go, ma'am."

Again she did not resist. Her hands loosened their grip and she turned. The actions caused the tattered dress to slide from her slim body. Her green eyes held Edge's gaze in a level stare and she made no attempt to cover the nakedness he had already seen and rejected.

"You have good reason to shame me again, sinner?" she asked.

"Twenty-five thousand of them," he replied, balling up the dress and stuffing it between two cases of blasting powder on the wagon. "This is what you do."

He told her only once, speaking softly, as he uncapped some bottles of whiskey and poured the liquor over the wagon. She nodded her understanding. Up at the top of the street, the prisoner returned to awareness with an agonised scream.

"If I do this, you will not kill Angel Francis?" she asked dully.

The half-breed grinned, guessing from her concern that she had seen the Earthly Angel with the pock-marked face among the survivors. "If you don't do it, the redskins'll kill the whole band of angels," he rasped. "Time's running out as fast as the blood of that guy up there." He jerked his thumb.

"I will do as you ask and pray that you will show mercy."

"Just pray that those indians are boozed enough to fall for this," he answered.

She ran around the front of the team, hesitated at the corner of the barn, then stepped out into the street. Edge climbed up on to the back of the wagon, tossed the Winchester on to the flat roof of the barn and then hauled himself aloft. In a crouch, he ran on a diagonal line, and stretched out flat above the doorway of the church section. He glanced up the street in time to see a knife slash downwards, severing one of Joseph's ears. The man screamed. A gasp of horror snapped the half-breed's attention to the street immediately below him. Sarah stood in front of the doorway, petrified by the ghastly sight of the torture victim.

"Just watching him ain't helping him," Edge encouraged softly coldly.

She glanced up at him and seemed on the brink of nausea again. He saw her release the catch on the door before he withdrew a few inches, into cover from the street.

"Please stop it!" she shrieked. "Please, if you stop this, I offer myself to you. Take me instead of . . . "

A dozen knives were sent spinning towards the screaming Joseph. The sound of Sarah's voice had silenced the yells of the Spokan indians as they whirled to look down the slope of the street. Perhaps for a moment they thought the rot-gut whiskey had driven them into delirium: caused their ears and eyes to play tricks on them. But then they recovered, shaking their heads and blinking at the reality of the nubile nakedness of the woman. The knives were loosed as the indians launched into a powerful run. Joseph's scream was curtailed and he folded forward over the stocks. A quivering cluster of knife handles seemed to be growing from his crimson-sheened back.

Fear constricted the women's throat, choking off the words. Just as the indians had been held immobile for a fragment of time, so Sarah felt herself rooted to the spot by the awesome sight of the sprinting men. Some were already as naked as she. Others hurled away the bottles and tore their breech cloths from their sweat-shined bodies as they ran. Then they began to shriek their crazed excitement. But, because the door to the church was just below him, Edge heard it as Sarah wrenched it open. Her bare feet slapped on the floorboards as she kicked off her shoes to race through the barn.

The indians were too drunk on liquor and the prospect of rape to give a thought to the possibillty of a trap. They shrieked more powerfully as they darted in through the open doorway. A lone Spokan saw the truth. He had tripped over his own discarded breech cloth. As he stumbled, fell, then picked himself up, he saw the tall figure of Edge rise erect on the roof.

"Chasing a white woman's bad medicine," the half-breed muttered.

The Winchester cracked and the indian spun back to the ground, blood gouting from his punctured heart. But Edge hit the street before the dead man, powering into a leap. He maintained his balance and whirled, slamming the door closed and crashing home the latch. Then he spun around again, to race along the front of the barn. Gunfire exploded and splinters of wood were torn from the corner as he ducked into its cover.

"It's the sonofabitch from the gorge!" Gabb yelled.

The naked Sarah was ten yards clear of the wagon-blocked entrance at the end of the barn. Her blonde hair streamed out behind her and sweat greased her exposed flesh. Two indians squeezed out around the side of the wagon to lunge in pursuit.

Edge pulled up short, squeezed the rifle trigger, levered the action and squeezed again. The indians screamed and sprawled to the ground, twitching into their death throes.

Edge grinned. "Hard way to go," he muttered as the aroused men ejaculated as the final act of their lives.

Many of the indians had been pulled up short by the crack of the Winchester and slam of the door as the first of their number died. Now others skidded to a halt at the sight of the bodies slumped beside the wagon. Gabb and Mackinlay poured lead at the corner around which Edge had raced. For a few moments, the half-breed was vulnerable. The Winchester was crooked under his arm and the Colt was still holstered as he took matches from his pocket, struck one, dropped the flaring stick into the box and hurled it towards the wagon.

He saw Sarah catch her foot in a hole and pitch forward. She yelled in alarm, fell and started to roll. She turned over and over through the prickly, blackened stubble of a burned wheat field.

Edge used the Colt to send a warning shot into the open doorway of the barn. Then he whirled, waited for a pause in the gunfire from the trappers, and lunged forward. He burst on to the open street in a crouching run. Then he dived into a forward roll. Yelling, Gabb and Mackinlay poured lead at him. Dust puffed and dirt spurted around him. He powered upright and plunged through the stable doorway. Horses and the ponies of the Spokan snorted and reared, spooked by his abrupt entry. Bullets thudded against the doorposts, erupting splinters.

The indians realised the significance of the fire on the wagon and vented their fear as they raced back through the church section of the barn. Sweating, his chest rising and falling as he regained his breath, the half-breed was crouched well back from the open doorway of the stable. His hooded eyes looked through the shower of bullet-exploded wood, showing no expression in their clear blueness as he saw the fire take hold. Shoulders thudded against the latched doorway across the street. A bullet whined through the stable doorway and drilled into the brain of a Spokan pony. The team hitched to the wagon smelled the smoke and reared to race away.

The powder exploded.

Edge's eyes narrowed even more against the hot blast. For a moment his vision was blurred. When it cleared, he saw the ripped-apart carcasses of the six-horse team raining down across the charred fields of the valley. The barn was engulfed in a thick, swirling cloud of black smoke. The gigantic roar of the explosion had deafened him and he could not hear the terrified squealing of the panicked horses and ponies as he stepped into the stable doorway.

He looked first to his right, and saw the white form of Sarah pressed against the blackness of the wheat field. He didn't know if she was alive or dead. Then he concentrated upon the scene of devastation across the street as the smoke was sucked away into the evening sky. The barn was unrecognisable for what it had been. Not a wall remained standing. And the stores it had once contained were almost completely destroyed. Even the great stones cut to build the cathedral had been blasted to smithereens and scattered. Blast and searing flame had killed the indians. Flying, bullet-paced fragments of stone had ripped their blackened bodies to pieces.

"Oh, you lousy, rotten, stinking bloody bastard!"

The half-breed's hearing returned to normal in time to discern the agonised tirade shouted at him by Gabb. Both trappers had been flung twenty yards by the blast. Something had ripped Mackinlay's head from his shoulders. His body lay crumpled in the middle of the street. Gabb had been hurled against the front of a house. His back looked broken. There was a great, crimson-smeared hole where his right arm had once been attached to his body. The ripped off piece of him lay five yards away, the festered hand still fisted around the rifle barrel.

"Weren't nothing personal, feller," Edge said as he approached the terribly injured man. "You shouldn't have got between me and the money I'm owed."

Shuffling footsteps sounded as the Earthly Angels emerged from hiding and moved slowly into town, staring blankly at the blackened ruin of the barn and the mutilated corpses.

"The Lord has ordained this!" Arch-Angel Luke intoned.

"See, it wasn't me," Edge said to Gabb as the trapper closed his eyes and the death rattle sounded in his throat. He spat, clearing the blast-driven dust from his throat. "Feller with a lot more willpower than me disarmed you."

CHAPTER EIGHT

"Go!" Hedges breathed, and went first.

Forrest and Seward sprinted after him, racing down the slope and hurling themselves behind the slumped carcasses of dead sheep. Scott, Bell and Rhett blasted covering fire at the corner of the monastery wall. Douglas cursed and nursed his shattered arm. Two wild, unaimed shots whined from where the Rebels waited. Each man in the advance trio spotted the next animal for his cover and lunged towards it. The troopers behind them blasted the Rebels again. Then the rôles were reversed as the men on the slope provided covering fire for those behind them to break from the trees.

The man in command of the Confederate infantry had chosen to keep his unit in a single group behind the solid cover of the wall. And it was only from this point that an occasional shot was exploded in answer to the barrage from the slope.

Only once was the advance on the monastery halted, while the troopers reloaded their weapons, huddling up close to the still-warm carcasses of the dead sheep, hearing the thud of bullets into the unfeeling meat which protected them. Then a fusillade of shots drove the Rebels back into cover and the troopers spurted closer to their objective, gaining the higher, more solid protection of dead cattle. The final run was across level ground to the inset doorway of the monastery. They arrived there breathless and sweating, shoulders slumped and mouths gaping. The exertion of the advance had drained them of their final reserves of stamina. But the lines of alertness were etched into their drawn faces and their eyes were bright, their trigger fingers poised. The knowledge that death lurk around the angle of the monastery wall, no more than thirty yards away, overrode the bone-deep exhaustion that demanded relief.

The blue eyes of Captain Hedges were the brightest and he knew he could rely on the men not to submit to physical needs now. For they, like him, were drawing strength from the exhilaration of the minor skirmish: the excitement of anticipating the killing to be done.

"Sergeant, Seward, Rhett," he whispered. "Go around. Scott, Bell, blast the corner from here. Keep it chest high. Corporal—"

"Jesus, sir, I'm sufferin'," Douglas moaned, sagging into a crouch.

"Do it in silence," Hedges hissed. "Unless you see this door open. Then yell your damn head off. Go."

He dropped to all fours and crawled out of the cover of the doorway arch. Above him, the Spencers of Scott and Bell cracked. Forrest sprinted away with the two troopers assigned to him. A head had appeared at the corner, but was hurriedly withdrawn as the rifle fire exploded lead towards it.

Hedges speeded his progress, uncomfortably aware of the stream of bullets cracking a few inches above his arched back. His lungs felt close to bursting with the effort and his vision was blurred by the salty sweat beads that dripped from his brow into his narrowed eyes. He glanced up the slope. The distance to the trees seemed enormous compared with the length of wall he had to crawl. He realised how much the spurting advance had sapped him. Incredibly, up there in the shade of the trees, a half dozen sheep which had survived the slaughter were grazing peacefully, impervious to the barrage of gunfire below them.

He stopped four feet back from the corner. The Spencers of Scott and Bell were fired empty and there was a short pause as they drew their Confederate Colts. A Rebel infantryman appeared abruptly at the corner. He had no reason to look down as he sent a shot cracking along the wall. Hedges cursed under his breath. He had been waiting for the sergeant and two troopers to open fire from the rear of the monastery. But the Rebel saw his squatting form and opened his mouth to shout a warning. Hedges put a bullet between the gaping lips and powered forward. He rose up under the crimson curve of gushing blood from the mouth of the toppling man. For a moment he froze, flattened against the wall. A single revolver shot whined across in front of him.

"You crazy?" Bell shrieked, knocking down Scott's gun hand.

Hedges groaned from the pain in his shoulder as he pushed away from the wall. He swung around the corner.

They were kids, all of them. The corporal was maybe eighteen. The two dead soldiers and the seven more who had moments to live could be no older than sixteen. New recruits flung into a war the Confederacy was losing, their uniforms still stiff from the quartermaster's store. Hedges blasted two of them in the stomach as their horrified eyes swung towards him after staring at the body with the smashed mouth.

The Captain was a more terrifying sight. Filthy dirty, heavily stubbled, his clothing still plastered to his powerful body from the two plunges into the river, he was the first Union soldier they had seen close to. He smelled of death and death glittered in the narrowed eyes; was snarled at them by the set of the lips curled back over his teeth.

In unison, the boy soldiers flung their rifles to the turf and thrust their arms high. At that moment, Forrest, Seward and Rhett lunged around the far corner at the rear of the monastery, Hedges saw the levelled guns and the grins of triumph splitting the faces of the men behind them. He knew the sound of his voice would not reach the troopers in time.

"Bye, kids," he snapped, and hurled himself back into the cover of the corner.

The youngsters in their stiff new uniforms had a moment to register surprise. Then the guns of the three troopers behind them exploded in a lethal hail of lead. Three of the young Rebels were hit in the back. Two whirled to take bullets in the chest and head as the second volley was loosed. All of them staggered away from the corner to collapse at the feet of Hedges. One of them looked up at the impassive figure of the tall Captain.

"My Ma!" he moaned. "Tell her I did my best for the South."

"Ain't got the time for women talk, kid," Hedges hissed.

The boy coughed, and spewed blood from a punctured lung. Heavy footfalls thudded on the turf and the three Union men skidded to a halt to grin down at their victims.

"Hey, one here still breathing, sarge," Rhett exclaimed, resting the muzzle of his Spencer against the throat of a boy Hedges had shot in the stomach.

"Sometimes you're good news, trooper," the Captain rasped, stepping forward to knock the rifle away.

"We got enough problems without prisoners!" Forrest snarled.

Hedges ignored him as he crouched beside the injured boy. He rested his rifle and drew the razor. The youngster eyed him with pathetic pleading.

"You're going to die, kid," Hedges said softly. "Easy or hard. Your choice. Somebody go for help?"

The Rebel was trying to stem the blood flow from his holed stomach. The crimson oozed between his interlocked fingers. "I ain't talkin'!" he grasped.

"Undo his pants," Hedges instructed.

"I'll do it!" Rhett volunteered.

"Who else?" Forrest growled.

"What you gonna do?" the Rebel whined as he felt the New Englander's fingers fumbling with his belt buckle.

"Geld you," Hedges answered nonchalantly.

"The lieutenant!" the boy shrieked. "Lieutenant James. He went. Told us to stay here and keep you pinned down until he brought in some cavalry from Baker's Crossin'."

He shrieked as Rhett groped into the front of his pants.

"How long will it take?" Hedges demanded evenly.

"They gotta be on their way here by now, mister." He shrieked again as Rhett exposed him.

When he raised his head to look down his body at the excited New Englander, Hedges slid the razor into his skull—into the flesh under his ear and penetrating the brain. He sighed and fell inert.

"I told him it'd be easy, Rhett," Hedges said as he stood up.

"Sure didn't go out hard," the New Englander muttered, releasing the dead boy's limp member.

"Captain!" Scott yelled.

Hedges picked up his Spencer, sheathed the razor and led the way wearily back towards the monastery entrance. The big door was open and three monks stood on the threshold. Their earnest faces just patches of paleness within the dark shadows of their cowls. They ignored the levelled revolvers of Scott and Bell.

"This is a closed order," the monk in the centre announced. "We do not admit strangers to our retreat. The soldiers respected our wishes."

"Changing the order, feller," Hedges told him, again aware of the pain in his shoulder. "Need medical attention, food and rest."

"I beseech you not to break with tradition!" the spokesman implored, his voice rising. "No one has ever——"

"It's wartime!" Hedges spat. "Old orders change. Get out of the damn way. Even monks have to get into new habits."

Lieutenant James pointed down at the monastery fifty minutes later. Beside him a cavalry captain eyed the peaceful scene with grim suspicion. Behind the two officers, a unit of thirty troopers awaited orders, calming their horses which sensed death in the warm, midday air. After a few moments, the captain beckoned a forward move and the horses were held to a walk down the sloping turf. Sheep and two surviving cows scuttled out of the path of the jingling cavalrymen. As they circled around to the front of the monastery, the men saw the splashes of brown, dried blood staining the turf.

"There was a fight, sir," the lieutenant said needlessly.

"Yeah, and who won it?" the cavalry captain muttered, wiping sweat from his chin.

"The soldiers put the enemy into full retreat."

Thirty rifles were drawn from saddle boots and trained at the opening door of the monastery. Three monks in enveloping habits stood in the entrance, faces hooded by the cowls. Behind them, on the lawned quadrangle, were heaped the carcasses of the slaughtered animals.

"What happened, father abbot?" the infantry officer asked, his tone reverent.

"The intruders slaughtered our beasts for cover. But your men retaliated well, sir. The intruders withdrew to the trees. Then they circled the basin and went north. Your men gave chase."

The grim-faced cavalry officer surveyed the basin and shook his head. "Don't seem likely."

"The father abbot wouldn't lie, sir!" Lieutenant James said, shocked.

"Maybe not, but I'm going to check out this place."

"We are a closed order!" The father abbot's voice was heavy with emotion—perhaps fear.

"I protest, sir!" James interjected as the senior officer made to heel his horse forward.

"Noted," the cavalryman snapped, and started his horse. The troopers in Rebel grey trailed him.

As instructed, the three monks moved to the side of the entrance and no further. So the father abbot remained firmly in the gun sight of Hedges' Spencer. The Captain was crouched in fetid concealment beneath the heap of animal carcasses. All his concentration was centred upon the father abbot.

"The friars are at prayer in the sanctuary chapel."

Hedges ignored the troopers and the troopers ignored the father abbot's cry. Commands were snapped and the men dismounted and began to search. Pale faced, expressing tacit concern, the infantry lieutenant remained mounted beyond the confines of the monastery. Once he seemed on the point of saying something—perhaps to apologise for the sacrilegious actions of the others. But he held his peace.

The search took less than thirty minutes. Then the troopers emerged into the sunlit quadrangle again and mounted their horses.

"Maybe I'll pay for this on Judgment Day," the Captain allowed as he moved his horse into the entrance gap and halted. "But desperate situations call for desperate measures."

"It is the same for both combatants," the father abbot replied ruefully. "We must all pray for peace."

"Some of us gotta fight for it!" the Captain growled, and gave the signal for his men to follow him out.

When the back markers cantered through, riding two abreast, the monks flanking the father abbot moved quickly forward to push the big door closed.

Hedges rose, using his good shoulder to heave a dead sheep clear so that he could climb out into the open.

"Let's go to chapel, fellers," he said, jerking the Spencer for the trio to lead the way.

They moved across the quadrangle and through an arched entrance into a cloister. A doorway at the far end gave on to the cool gloom of the chapel. At least fifty monks knelt with their heads bowed, incanting a prayer in a low monotone.

"Okay!" Hedges yelled. "Here endeth the one hundred and first lesson in survival."

The genuine monks ignored the raucous tones of the Captain, continuing with their prayers. The six Union troopers rose, tossing their heads to shake off the cowls. Each dirt-streaked, unshaven face was split by a grin of relief.

"Lousy service, Captain," Forrest said against the mumbling of massed voices calling softly for him to be forgiven. "Deadly sermon."

He shoved the kneeling figure next to him. It toppled, banged into the next one, and the chain reaction continued down the line. Within moments, the clerically-robed bodies of the Rebel infantrymen were all sprawled on the chapel's stone floor.

"No!" Angel Sarah screamed.

The stoic eyes of the citizens of Paradise all moved their gaze from their immediate surroundings to look towards the woman. She was running in from the burnt wheatfield, her nude body only white in patches now. For the most part, she was covered with the soot and ash of the destroyed crop.

Edge merely glanced at her as she staggered into the street between the stable and the blasted barn. Then he raked his narrowed eyes over the group of black-garbed Earthly Angels.

"Cover yourself!" Luke roared, his voice quivering with shock as he realised the woman was naked.

"Francis!" Edge called softly, and the man with the acned face turned to look at the half-breed.

"Warned you, feller," Edge reminded him as he levelled the Winchester. "A man's allowed one mistake. You used up yours pointing that Starr musket at me. Picking my pocket was one too many. Will of Edge."

He squeezed the trigger of the rifle. The bullet drilled into the man's chest. He was less than fifteen feet from the muzzle. The impact of the lead lifted him off his feet and hurled him backwards. Those around him stood in almost rigid acceptance of the new death in their town. Only those who were brushed by the falling body rocked slightly.

Sarah halted abruptly, stood for a moment, then collapsed to her knees and fell, sobbing, to the ground.

"Take the twenty-five grand now, feller," the half-breed said to Luke.

He was as unmoved as everybody but Sarah by the cold-blooded killing of Francis. "We took one thousand two hundred dollars from you in payment of your fine," he said evenly.

"The sooted-up angel offered me the whole bundle to get rid of your visitors," Edge said. "Fulfilled my end of the deal. They sure blew town."

"And I fear you must leave empty-handed, sinner," Luke replied. He raised an arm to point towards the blackened ruin of the barn. "Like Angel Francis, I made a mistake. When the invaders came, I took the cathedral fund into the church for safe-keeping. I regret that, in the haste to leave, I forget about the money." He sighed in resignation. "Will you kill me, too?"

A momentary rage took hold of Edge as he stared along the pointing arm of the white-haired man. He had no doubt that Luke was speaking the truth. If he could accept death so coldly, the loss of mere money—even twenty-five thousand dollars—would mean little to him. Then the fury drained out of him. He had been on the threshold of riches many times before, only to be cheated by a twist of fate as cruel as he was. There would be no satisfaction in further killing. Not of these people who seemed to welcome death as a coveted reward of good living.

They would all pay for Luke's mistake the hard way: toiling to reclaim the burnt-out land and raising new crops to earn money for the cathedral. He canted the Winchester across his shoulder.

"No deal, feller," he said slowly. "I don't owe this town any favours."

He looked towards the south west. California lay in that direction. He'd been making that way when he came upon the trappers. There was nothing now to stop him moving on again. Perhaps he would find some peace there this time. Last time there had been none.* But a man like Edge had little more than hope and fast reflexes going for him.

"I see Paradise flowering again!" the diminuitive Prohet Thomas announced shrilly, spreading his short arms to the skies. "I see the great cathedral thrusting up from fields of golden wheat. Our spiritual and bodily needs will be fulfilled in abundance."

"But how?" somebody demanded. "How can we begin? We have no seed and no money to buy it."

"We do not need much," Luke said, warming to the small man's vision. "We must go out from Paradise and beg for the little we need."

"But it must be done speedily," Prophet Thomas urged. "The crops must be sown before spring is over."

"Why don't you just bundle up the little guy and sell him?" Edge said with a wry smile as he turned to go into the timber for his horse.

"What's that, sinner?" the near midget of a man called.

"You folks being in such an all-fired hurry," the half-breed replied as he ambled across the street. "For a small prophet you ought to get a quick return."

**See—Edge: California Killing.*

NEL BESTSELLERS

Crime			
T027 821	GAUDY NIGHT	*Dorothy L. Sayers*	75p
T030 180	UNNATURAL DEATH	*Dorothy L. Sayers*	60p
T026 663	THE DOCUMENTS IN THE CASE	*Dorothy L. Sayers*	50p
Fiction			
T029 522	HATTER'S CASTLE	*A. J. Cronin*	£1.00
T030 199	CRUSADER'S TOMB	*A. J. Cronin*	£1.25
T031 276	THE CITADEL	*A. J. Cronin*	95p
T029 158	THE STARS LOOK DOWN	*A. J. Cronin*	£1.00
T022 021	THREE LOVES	*A. J. Cronin*	90p
T022 536	THE HARRAD EXPERIMENT	*Robert H. Rimmer*	50p
T022 994	THE DREAM MERCHANTS	*Harold Robbins*	95p
T023 303	THE PIRATE	*Harold Robbins*	95p
T022 986	THE CARPETBAGGERS	*Harold Robbins*	£1.00
T031 667	WHERE LOVE HAS GONE	*Harold Robbins*	£1.00
T023 958	THE ADVENTURERS	*Harold Robbins*	£1.00
T031 659	THE INHERITORS	*Harold Robbins*	95p
T031 586	STILETTO	*Harold Robbins*	60p
T025 268	NEVER LEAVE ME	*Harold Robbins*	50p
T025 292	NEVER LOVE A STRANGER	*Harold Robbins*	90p
T022 226	A STONE FOR DANNY FISHER	*Harold Robbins*	80p
T031 640	79 PARK AVENUE	*Harold Robbins*	80p
T027 945	THE BETSY	*Harold Robbins*	90p
T031 241	EVENING IN BYZANTIUM	*Irwin Shaw*	75p
T029 557	RICH MAN, POOR MAN	*Irwin Shaw*	£1.25
Historical			
T023 079	LORD GEOFFREY'S FANCY	*Alfred Duggan*	60p
T024 903	THE KING OF ATHELNEY	*Alfred Duggan*	60p
T023 125	FOX 11: FIRESHIP	*Adam Hardy*	35p
T024 946	FOX 12: BLOOD BEACH	*Adam Hardy*	35p
T027 651	FOX 13: SEAFLAME	*Adam Hardy*	40p
Science Fiction			
T029 492	STRANGER IN A STRANGE LAND	*Robert Heinlein*	80p
T029 484	I WILL FEAR NO EVIL	*Robert Heinlein*	95p
T031 462	DUNE	*Frank Herbert*	£1.25
T022 854	DUNE MESSIAH	*Frank Herbert*	60p
War			
T027 066	COLDITZ: THE GERMAN STORY	*Reinhold Eggers*	50p
T025 438	LILLIPUT FLEET	*A. Cecil Hampshire*	50p
T026 299	TRAWLERS GO TO WAR	*Lund & Ludlam*	50p
Western			
T020 754	EDGE 15: BLOOD RUN	*George Gilman*	35p
T022 706	EDGE 16: THE FINAL SHOT	*George Gilman*	35p
T024 881	EDGE 17: VENGEANCE VALLEY	*George Gilman*	40p
General			
T021 009	SEX MANNERS FOR MEN	*Robert Chartham*	35p
T023 206	THE BOOK OF LOVE	*Dr David Delvin*	90p
T028 828	THE LONG BANANA SKIN	*Michael Bentine*	90p

NEL P.O. BOX 11. FALMOUTH TR10 9EN, CORNWALL.
For U.K.: Customers should include to cover postage, 19p for the first book plus 9p per copy for each additional book ordered up to a maximum charge of 73p.
For B.F.P.O. and Eire: Customers should include to cover postage, 19p for the first book plus 9p per copy for the next 6 and thereafter 3p per book
For Overseas: Customers should include to cover postage, 20p for the first book plus 10p per copy for each additional book.

Name ______________________________

Address ______________________________

____

Title ______________________________
(JULY)

Whilst every effort is made to maintain prices, new editions or printings may carry an increased price and the actual price of the edition supplied will apply.